T5-CQE-119

GEORGE BAILEY has been an on-the-scene observer of the East–West conflict since World War II, when he served as US Army liaison officer to the Red Army. He was present as interpreter/translator at the surrender negotiations in Reims and Berlin.

After the war he was a resettlement officer for Soviet Army defectors, and a liaison officer with the Soviet Army and German police in Berlin. As the Cold War escalated, he was ABC's resident correspondent in Berlin and Vienna, covering growing tensions in Eastern Europe. In 1959 he was honored with the Overseas Press Club's Award for best magazine reporting on foreign affairs.

George Bailey has been correspondent and executive editor of *The Reporter*, has worked for Axel Springer Verlag Berlin as editor, special correspondent, and liaison officer, was coordinating editor of *Kontinent* magazine, and his news commentary has been featured in the American, British, and German press. He is the author of several books including *Kontinent 4: Contemporary Russian Writers, Germans,* and *Munich*, with the editors of *Time*. He has been a frequent panelist on German and Austrian television.

Other Avon and Discus Books by
George Bailey

GERMANS
KONTINENT 4: CONTEMPORARY RUSSIAN WRITERS

ARMAGEDDON IN PRIME TIME

George Bailey

 AVON
PUBLISHERS OF BARD, CAMELOT, DISCUS AND FLARE BOOKS

ARMAGEDDON IN PRIME TIME is an original publication of Avon Books. This work has never before appeared in book form.

AVON BOOKS
A division of
The Hearst Corporation
1790 Broadway
New York, New York 10019

First Avon Printing, November, 1984

AVON TRADEMARK REG. U.S. PAT. OFF AND IN OTHER COUNTRIES, MARCA REGISTRADA, HECHO EN U.S.A.

Printed in the U.S.A.

WFH 10 9 8 7 6 5 4 3 2 1

To Fifikus

ACKNOWLEDGMENTS

To the staff of Radio Liberty

ARMAGEDDON IN PRIME TIME

Chapter I

"We are coming to the end of the world. Presidents and ministers are eating each other up. Military men are traitors. Society is corrupt. The privileged, the notables are not worried about the poor...." It need not have taken, as in this instance, an Iranian terrorist subchieftain in Beirut to say as much on the threshold of the Orwellian year 1984. The press and the media in general—East and West, in the neutral countries, and in the Third World at large—were saying the same thing. "The fate of mankind—salvation or destruction—still lies in the hands of the atomic superpowers," wrote the *Tagesspiegel* (*Daily Mirror*) of Berlin on New Year's Day. "The hopes of the peoples of the world that the negotiations in Geneva over a limitation of medium-range rockets would lead to an agreement have been smashed in the course of the year just ended.... In the coming periods (who knows how long?) lies hidden the answer to the anxious question—how will all this end?"

So now at last we have it, and right on time: the world divided in accordance with George Orwell's prophetic nightmare into two camps, each equipped with atomic weapons capable of unimaginable destruction, each apparently bent on destroying the other—1984! For the first time in the history of the globe as a whole the conventional greeting "Happy New Year!" sounded like the worst kind of sarcasm.

The confrontation between the Soviet Union and the United States is not only the great confrontation of our time but arguably the greatest confrontation of all time—past, present, and future. Its resolution will predictably usher in or prelude some sort of cogent world order. This is not to prophesy the coming of eternal peace; there may well be coups d'état galore, insurrections, and rebellions, perhaps of whole continents, occurring at various intervals stretching into the infinite future. But it is categorically improbable that there shall ever again be on this planet another such massive shaping up and glacially gradual opposition of two superpowers on either side of the two great oceans. The chances are that this is it. Once and for all.

The immediate cause of this confrontation was the Second World War, the immediate cause of which in turn was the First World War via its monstrous progeny the Third Reich. It is misleading to say that the Germans lost World War II, without adding that the Second World War, like the First, was basically two wars and the Germans lost them both. In World War I the Germans lost the war on the western front but won the war on the eastern front. The loss of World War II on both fronts was a novum in German history, and it sealed the division of Germany.

In his book *Russia and History's Turning Point*, Aleksandr Kerensky articulates the view that World War II was in reality merely a continuation of World War I—a more active phase, one might say, after a lull in the fighting that lasted, and then fitfully, for only nineteen years while the opposing sides caught their breath and rearmed and equipped themselves. One can apply the same logic to the postwar period of World

War II, turning around Clausewitz's dictum that war is a continuation of politics by other means.

After World War II what looked like a series of free choices—the Western Allies' decision to arm West Germany and the Soviet decision to arm East Germany, the Soviet decision to build a wall through the middle of Berlin and the Western Allies' "decision" to accept it, for examples—was in reality a progression of foregone conclusions stemming from the central fact of Germany's loss of the two wars in 1945. When the two fronts of the opposing world systems, capitalism and communism, which were united only in their opposition to Germany, came together in the center of Germany in the historic meeting on the Elbe, the result was not a meeting but a confrontation; it had to be. When the fronts met, they automatically coalesced into the Iron Curtain by virtue of the fact that the opposing systems had together succeeded in destroying the only thing that had forced their association in the first place.

The problem is further complicated by the deterioration of basic elements in the foundations of society, both national and international—community and comity. When Friedrich Nietzsche announced the death of God in the late nineteenth century, he was summing up a series of phenomena that had already taken place and were destined to continue into the indefinite future: the separation of church and state; the decrease in the influence of the congregation in society; the equivalence of modernization to secularization; the loosening, if not indeed the destruction, of the family as the basic ethical unit in society, to name but a few. Aleksandr Solzhenitsyn in his Templeton Award speech in the Guild Hall of London in 1983, "We Have Forgotten God," put the onset of this forgetfulness at 300 years ago. He traced most of the ills of modern society to this fact. This is particularly interesting insofar as the postulates of secularization as an enlightening, humanistic process have themselves become questionable. Solzhenitsyn himself is the chief "hostile interrogator" of secularism as humanism.

Yet the deterioration in comity and community is by

no means limited to the church and the scope of its influence. The classic consensus supporting the market economy which is the linchpin of the liberal democratic society is also very much in contention. So long as there was apparent equality in the subordination of everyone to the laws of the marketplace as the rationale of allegiance to the political system (conventional Western democracy), all was well. But this consensus began to crumble at least a century ago. Beginning then, more and more citizens of Western industrial societies ceased to see themselves as equal in their opportunities to make the most of a free market in a free society. The rise and development of socialism in Europe is the most basic but not the only form of this questioning. Perhaps most significantly, it was an increasingly secularized Protestant clergy that first began, and continues foremost, to regard the very postulates of a market society as morally wrong.

In today's world there are question marks everywhere. With the Reformation there began an unremitting accumulation of questions paving the way, so it is recorded, for the Enlightenment and the rise of the bourgeoisie. It was the countermovement to the rise of the bourgeoisie—socialism and Marxism—that attacked the very tenets of the bourgeois commercial ethic. Marxism in particular questioned the very meanings of the words used by the bourgeoisie, denying the sincerity of their usage as well as the validity of their concepts. Marxists began to use words in their own way, ascribing their own, partisan meanings as they saw fit.

Hand in hand with the deliberate piracy of words and their definitions by the Marxists (and, above all, by the Soviets) went the undeliberate industrialization of language that accompanied the industrial revolution, an aspect of both growth and decay that is largely overlooked by historians.

The onset of the industrial revolution—for example, the invention of the steam engine and the railroad— fired the imagination of poets and writers in an unprecedented way. It was dream come true. As the German poet Novalis, who was by profession a mining assessor, put it in 1795, "The commercial spirit is the world spirit. It is the most magnificent spirit altogether, setting everything in motion and combining everything. It begets countries and cities, nations and works of art." There is nothing, as Wyndham Lewis has told us, which is so attractive to the romantic spirit, so full of "the pungent illusion of life," as commerce in general and the industrial revolution in particular.

Perhaps the most startling and ominous confusion of definitions and concepts is the result of the nuclear stalemate itself. Against its background the very concepts of war and peace have become confused. In a nuclear age all military action must be kept below the threshold of the commitment of nuclear weapons. We no longer have mobilizations, nor do we have declarations of war; there have been a good many wars (forty-four going on at this writing) since World War II but not a single declaration of war.

Of course, the "decision at Nuremberg" played a role here, too, in outlawing aggressive wars. Any nation declaring war today brands itself the aggressor. So in the stead of the aggressive war, there is the war of liberation, which can be easily camouflaged as a civil war fought by patriots or any other proxies as an act of international solidarity. The civil war of liberation brings with it of necessity commandos, guerrillas, in sum irregulars of all sorts—paramilitary (militia) and downright homegrown terrorists. The commando or guerrilla-terrorist is the exploiter par excellence of the confusion of concepts. He spreads confusion to mask his attack or uses an especially peaceful occasion in order to achieve maximum surprise (the Tet offensive; the "friendly" Olympic games in Munich; the Yom Kippur War). He attacks from ambush. The nature of the civil war of liberation makes it impossible for a conventional military force to assert itself in the field. The field is everywhere—which is to say, there is no field ("We can't win; they can't lose").

In the Nuremberg dock Colonel General Alfred Jodl tried to explain Hitler's Commando Order, which directed that all commandos were to be executed without

exception, regardless of their actions. As he put it—
and he was putting it mildly—"many of the British
commandos were acting in an illegal fashion and thus
placing themselves outside military law." But then, who
had put commandos *inside* military law? By their very
nature commandos constitute a borderline case. They
are partisans in uniform or, rather, uniformed and
highly trained troops acting as partisans.

The commandos in World War II were a British innovation. Hitler condemned the innovation out of hand,
outlawing the commandos a priori. Although Jodl refused point-blank to draft the Commando Order, he was
obliged to distribute the order or resign. But he took
steps to limit its application to troops that had acted
"in an unsoldierly fashion." Thus he accepted the innovation of commandos per se but attempted to circum-
scribe it by insisting on the strict adherence to formal
rules. Still, the damage was done, and the judges at
Nuremberg confirmed it. The commandos were a borderline case; their acceptance by the Allied high court
blurred the rules, and with them the pertinent definition of words and concepts.

And there are reversals of concepts, such as Clausewitz's dictum that war is the continuation of politics by
other means. The view that politics, particularly international politics, was the continuation of war by other
means—namely, infiltration to begin with—was certainly Lenin's: "We must be able to agree to any sacrifice and even if need be to resort to all sorts of tricks,
slyness, illegal methods, evasion and concealment of
truth, only so as to get into the trade unions and to
remain in them and to carry on Communist work at all
costs."

Indeed, there are those, the émigré Russians among
them, who consider that World War III has already
begun. A good many Germans, more and more of them
as time goes on, would agree with them. Indeed, more
than a few would agree that World War III is merely
a continuation of World War II. What is the difference
between a commando and a terrorist who styles himself
a soldier of the Red Army Faction and insists on being

treated (if taken alive) as a prisoner of war? But then, society has changed radically since the time, some thirty years ago, when the death penalty was abolished in West Germany.

In his essay "Reflections on the Guillotine" Albert Camus has no trouble in demolishing the conventional justification for the death penalty—namely, that it is exemplary, that the state's exercise of the power over life and death acts as a deterrent. And in another famous essay on the use of terror by totalitarian regimes, Camus points out that such a regime has no choice but to murder more or less indiscriminately because only in this way can it bring the public to take it seriously.

Today's terrorists murder for the same reason. But whereas the state in Western countries in the last four decades has shamefacedly concealed its executions, today's organized and trained terrorists do everything they can to achieve maximum publicity for their "executions." Never in history has the spectacle of public executions achieved anything like its present dimensions at the hands of the terrorists. It is regarded against the background of the all-pervasive cult of violence in television, radio, and films. To this must be added the massive inadvertent cooperation of an increasingly sensationalist international press. There were some 5,000 journalists in Holland when a group of émigré Moluccans took a trainful of hostages. The topflight journalists of the world united in Holland because it was professionally safe to assume that so long as the Moluccan terrorists held the center of the world's stage, no other acts of terrorism would take place elsewhere.

Even before the terrorists seized on murder as the most effective instrument to impose their will on families, populations, and governments, the entertainment industry had seized on murder garishly displayed as the most effective means of pleasing the crowd. Apparently the only way the great inert mass of televiewers can feel that it is alive is to be confronted continually with the spectacle of violent death.

But there is much more. Modern technology has made the seizure of the power over life and death a comparatively simple matter. Whereas fifty years ago public buildings were constructed in the style of the Italian palazzo, which was a fortress, they are now constructed very largely out of glass. One man with a few bricks can bring down the side of a ten-story building. "People who live in glass houses shouldn't throw stones" runs the proverb. Well, people who live in glass houses should also see to it that there are no stones lying around in the streets. For the truth of the proverb is that a glass house is a provocation. And every boy is a stone thrower. One terrorist with a fake hand grenade can commandeer a jetliner. Modern technology has increased the leverage of the individual terrorist a thousandfold. So spectacular an increase in technical leverage is also a provocation.

Against this background the state, in many Western societies, has chosen to renounce its prerogative to inflict the death penalty in a general context in which the unofficial death penalty has become publicized and the means of inflicting it made more available than ever. Terrorists exploit this publicity to use murder as an instrument of political power with increasing effect. Not to mince words, they penalize the state by executing their hostages if the state fails to acquiesce to their demands. And the effective blackmail of a government is a political act as old as politics itself. In sum then, as regards the supreme privilege of society, the terrorists have stepped in where the state has stepped out.

It is important to realize the full consequences of this exchange of roles. The renunciation of the death penalty by the state deprives it not only of eliminating tried and convicted terrorist murderers, but also, by extension, of the means of imposing even so much as a moderately long prison sentence—witness the three convicted and sentenced Arab terrorists of the Black September in the Munich Olympic Games who were exchanged for a Lufthansa crew and passengers taken hostage by the Palestinians and the five convicted and sentenced German terrorists who were exchanged for Peter Lorenz, the mayor of Berlin, in 1969. The renunciation of the death penalty by the state and its arrogation by the terrorists undermine the criminal code and make a mockery of the system of justice as a whole. For this reason the West German state finally woke up to the fact that it had no choice but to refuse to exchange eleven German terrorists for Hans Martin Schleyer. In refusing this exchange, the German chancellor in effect condemned Schleyer to death at the hands of his terrorist captors.

The fact is that it has proved impossible to abolish the death penalty. If the power over life and death is given up by the state, it is given over, redoubled, into the hands of Everyman. For the power over life and death is in the nature of things. This is not an abstraction. It is the mark of Cain. It is merely a question of who inflicts the death penalty, and how and why. We regard as reactionary the contention that humankind is potentially savage and must be contained by the example of an effective death penalty. But what is to be said to the terrorists who demonstrate daily and in the bloodiest manner the correctness of this contention? *Si l'on veut abolir la peine de mort en ce cas, que MM. les assassins commencent.* [If one wishes to abolish the death penalty, then will the assassins be so kind as to begin?]

The mainspring of the terrorists' increasing violence is frustration. This results from the fact that the capitalist system contains so much freedom. It is extremely difficult to get outside the system in order to rebel against it. In a capitalist society the would-be rebel finds himself breaking butterflies on the wheel and using a battering ram against open doors. This is why the capitalist or modern industrial free enterprise system is in itself a provocation—a provocation to violence. For only physical violence is strong enough or extravagant enough to attract notice or to register at all within the vast framework of the system.

So the progression of the Baader-Meinhof gang in West Germany from setting fire to department stores, to planting bombs in public buildings, robbing banks, and then killing outright for a declared political purpose is clear and comprehensible. For the only violence that really registers is that done to the human body.

Violence done to accepted form is no longer practically possible or even meaningful because the idea of accepted form is disappearing in our Western permissive society. Rebellion against accepted form has become nothing more than a change in fashion. A rebel against accepted form is simply a professional trading on the fashion of rebellion, and contributing to the fashion, not to the rebellion.

By stark contrast, it is very easy to get outside the Communist system. All the individual as an individual has to do in a Communist society is play it straight, doing what comes naturally, and he is in the soup. Censorship and the rules of prescribed conduct, public and private, are so strict that in the Soviet Union rebels are born, not made.

The Soviet Union has expanded the death penalty to include economic crimes, not done away with it altogether. Soviet dissidents in their own society are the counterparts of the terrorists in the West, counterparts and direct opposites because all that the dissidents in a Communist society have to do is speak up as individuals against the hideous abstraction of the collective and they are damned outright, exiled or deported, imprisoned, exchanged for Communist prisoners in the West, or hounded to death. It is indeed very easy.

What tremendous leverage a Soviet dissident with a command of language has! What damage to the Soviet system he can do! Aleksandr Solzhenitsyn wrote *The Gulag Archipelago* and affixed the mark of Cain on the forehead of the Soviet system. The Soviet dissidents exposed the Soviet system for what it is: a crude dictatorship run by a clique. In the Soviet system violence is done to the dissidents by the state; in the West violence is done to the state by the dissidents, who must turn to terrorism in order to make themselves known and to be taken seriously.

Efforts, such as the founding of the United Nations and its various branches, to relieve the confrontation, while not always entirely unsuccessful, resulted for the most part in the recreation of new arenas for the struggle. The UN was turned into a multinational diplomatic battleground within a year after the inaugural ceremony in San Francisco in 1945. The confrontation ramifies as it continues—even into joint efforts to avoid confrontation—especially in the arena of diplomacy. Here, too, a definition and a traditional concept have been undergoing a process of corruption for decades.

Ever since World War II intelligence agencies of the larger nations have been gradually superseding conventional diplomatic institutions. The work of maintaining or expanding positions of influence in foreign countries cannot be done only by diplomatic means. The global positions of both the United States and the Soviet Union are built on systems of military alliances. But the fact that the Soviet Union has invaded (or reinvaded, in the case of Hungary) two of its allies and bullied a third into declaring a state of war to exist within itself (as in the case of Poland) roughly within each succeeding decade of the last thirty years should not obscure the Soviet preference for managing such crises by political rather than military means. The significance of the fact that it could not salvage the Hungarian, Czechoslovak, and Polish situations politically (the Polish situation has by no means ended), let alone diplomatically, can hardly be exaggerated. (The point is that solving such situations militarily rather than politically is no solution at all. It can be argued with cogency that the privileged position Hungary enjoys vis-à-vis the Soviet Union at present is a direct result of the Hungarian Revolution and the Soviet handling of it.) But the Soviet inability to do so has placed all the more emphasis on intelligence work as the most effective means of political action in a foreign country.

The expulsion by Great Britain of 105 Soviet spy-diplomats in 1971 was unprecedented in the annals of diplomacy. But just ten years later, after almost a decade of "détente," Soviet "spyplomacy" was on the upsurge again. In 1981, 21 Soviet diplomats were expelled from their countries of assignment, in 1982 it was 48, and in 1983 the number had risen to the record-breaking 176. In France alone 47 diplomats were publicly named personae non gratae and obliged to leave the country forthwith. In actuality on this occasion France expelled more than 100 Soviets connected with the various Soviet foreign service missions in France but did not make their names or number known to the public. Throughout 1983 and well into 1984 hardly a week went by that some Soviet diplomats in some Western or neutral country weren't sent packing.

Indeed, the expulsions fell so rapidly that the Soviet Union had no time to retaliate except in the rarest of cases—or even officially to protest until at the turn of the year Bangladesh expelled a full dozen Soviets from its territory and scarcely ten days later Norway expelled nine Soviet diplomats in the wake of the country's worst spy scandal in its history. Arne Treholt, the Norwegian Foreign Affairs Office spokesman, had been under surveillance by Norwegian authorities for almost five years before his arrest. Soviet spy masters are not the most subtle in the world; they are frequently caught red-handed and generally easy to make out. But the large number of Soviet spy exposés is attributable as well to the fact that the Soviets believe in large numbers, in quantity rather than in quality, in espionage as in industrial production. The increasing number of expulsions of Soviet "diplomats" is also the result of an increasing number of host governments (and notably of small countries susceptible to various forms of Soviet pressure) simply deciding no longer to put up with the Eastern superpower's clubfooted shenanigans on their territory. Enough apparently is enough.

In the main diplomatic arena, the United Nations, the Soviets have clearly outstripped their rivals, the Americans. One of the reasons for the Soviets' superiority has been the willingness of the United States to accord special privileges to the Soviet Union, beginning with its agreeing to give the USSR three votes (with one each for the Ukraine and Byelorussia as separate states!). In addition, exceptions in procedure and protocol are made for the Soviets and often enough for their satellites.

There are, for example, 474 Soviet citizens who are

international civil servants employed by the UN secretariat, the administrative body of the organization.
Every workday the 474 are carried in a cavalcade of
buses from their compound in Riverdale, New York, to
United Nations headquarters in Manhattan and back
again at the close of work. By this means their opportunities for contacts outside the confines of the secretariat are virtually precluded. These and a number of
similar arrangements are in flat violation of the spirit
and the letter of the United Nations Charter, which
stipulates that no staff member "shall seek or receive
instructions from any government." Of course, the Soviet civil servants do nothing else but receive instructions from the Soviet government. The secretariat,
according to the Charter, is supposed to constitute a
group of civil servants without boundaries who remain
impartial in international disputes and loyal to the world
body itself.

The very fact that each of the Soviet United Nations
secretariat employees concerned is a member of the
Communist party of the Soviet Union is in itself a crass
violation of the terms of the organization's charter.
Membership in any Communist party, let alone that of
the USSR, binds the member to strict observance of the
principle of *partiinost'* ("party spirit") with the party.
Logically, then, the secretariat would have to insist
that only Soviet nonparty members become international civil servants in order to satisfy the terms of its
own charter.

Of course, the argument against enforcing the application of the terms of the charter to all members of
the secretariat is the immemorial one that it would
merely create trouble and bring no improvement. Thus
when, in spite of all precautionary measures, the Soviet
secretariat employee Vladimir Yakimetz requested and
received political asylum in the United States in February 1983, the Soviets insisted that he be forced to
leave. The United Nations secretary-general, Jovier
Pérez de Cuéllar, took the easy way out by refusing to
renew Yakimetz's contract when it expired at the beginning of 1984. Yakimetz appealed his case to the

United Nations Review Board for reinstatement. This temporary standoff symbolizes the Soviet situation in the secretariat and in the organization as a whole: The Soviets belong to the United Nations as full-fledged members, indeed, as cofounders—but on their terms.

Thus the confrontation between the two superpowers in the United Nations Organization is an unequal struggle. It is a struggle that has remained out of balance since the American invention and application of the atomic bomb. The A-bomb effectively ended World War II but simultaneously signaled the start of the nuclear arms race. The American atomic bomb was combined with the German V-2 rocket to produce the intercontinental ballistic missile (ICBM) and ushered in, after a brief period of American monopoly, the deadliest form of competition with the Soviet Union. (While other nations, such as Britain, France, and China, have the bomb and the necessary delivery systems, all have been effectively priced out of the nuclear arms race proper.)

The one constant in the military confrontation is the Soviet reliance on quantity, evidenced in the installation of hundreds of SS-22 intermediate missiles with multiple warheads first in Western European Russia, Byelorussia, and the Ukraine and later (as a demonstrative answer to the installation of Pershing and cruise missiles in Western Europe) in Czechoslovakia and East Germany, as well as in the fitting and commissioning of huge tank armies.

The Soviet Union has maintained a standing army of at least 3.2 million men ever since the end of World War II. Until the commitment of a force of approximately 100,000 men in Afghanistan in 1979, these troops were almost exclusively used to maintain a military presence in the satellites (except Romania and Bulgaria) or by conducting maneuvers on satellite territory or along their borders for purposes of psychological warfare.

It is no great conscious consolation that the unprecedented Soviet arms buildup throughout the seventies and into the eighties can be regarded as an attempt to compensate for the cosmic psychological impression of Neil Armstrong's foot on the moon as well as to capitalize on the paralysis of American national will in the wake of Watergate and the debacle in Vietnam. Perhaps the greatest shock for the Russians came when Paul Nitze announced at the beginning of the nuclear disarmament negotiations in Geneva in 1982 that the Soviets would either come to reasonable terms or be driven into the ground in an arms race with the United States. Thus the American economic recovery, already visible at the end of 1982, was as alarming to the Soviets as was the ease with which Ronald Reagan gained congressional approval for major arms projects.

For it is in the economic field that the Soviets have made their worst showing. Far from burying the United States in the field of economic competition in twenty years, as Nikita Khrushchev threatened and promised, the Soviet Union has gained few, if any, percentage points and has ruined whole sectors of its economy in the process. Indeed, in more than sixty-five years of communism the Soviet Union has still failed to produce so much as one single item or article, let alone an entire line of wares, that has made anything remotely resembling a breakthrough in the international market. The Kalashnikov machine gun is only a partial, qualified exception.

By any account the Soviet economic performance ranks from mediocre to miserable. The consequences of this failure—for such it unquestionably is—are many and varied, and their full significance is difficult to discern. By holy Marxist-Leninist writ the Communist system is the paradise of the workers and peasants, who, as fulfilled individuals in a classless, utopian society, achieve marvels of productivity. They easily outdo, in both quantity and quality, their unenlightened, unliberated brethren in capitalist countries who are the slaves of a historically outmoded and therefore backward society and political system. In more than sixtyfive years this has not happened. Indeed, something rather like the opposite has occurred. The Soviet Union has made some spectacular strides in science and technology: It was the first to put an artificial satellite into orbit and the first to put a human into space. But this was achieved by dint of extraordinary concentration of effort and hence the enforced neglect of many other sectors of the economy, notably and well-nigh disastrously of the most basic of all means of production: agriculture.

It would be difficult to exaggerate the force of the impact on domestic and world opinion of the Soviet failure in agriculture. Perhaps one of the standard Soviet jokes captures the fiasco as well as anything else: "Have you heard of the latest Soviet miracle? Well, we plant wheat in the Ukraine, and it comes up in Iowa!" Regardless of the views various experts take, the failure remains fundamental: Crop failures in the Soviet Union are only a matter of degree.

Beginning in 1976, the Soviet Union ceased publishing statistics of grain production. But by cross-reference and collation, fairly accurate estimates can be made. Thus in a good year—1983 (the first in the last five)—grain production was estimated at 200 million tons, which represents a shortfall of 40 million tons, or 20 percent, from the amount necessary to meet the Soviet Union's annual needs. In a bad year the shortfall has been at least half again as large—anywhere from 30 to 40 percent off. This is the kind of chronic deficit that everybody understands. To make it up, the Soviet Union is obliged to spend huge amounts of its hard-won and embarrassingly insufficient hard-currency reserves.

As a result, the agricultural deficit works restrictions on programs and policies across the board—including foreign policy. One of the reasons the Soviet Union could not maintain its privileged position in Egypt was the need to supply the United Arab Republic with 4 million tons of wheat each and every year. The USSR was simply incapable of producing enough wheat to spare the 4 million tons and was unwilling to buy as much more on the international market for the purpose of supplying Egypt. By extension, the agricultural failure adversely affects the entire area of Soviet foreign aid, even in the heavily favored sector of arms shipments. Arms shipments left aside, Soviet foreign aid is hardly more than token, making up hardly one-tenth of the American counterpart.

All dictatorships instinctively appreciate the special role of athletics as an occupation and preoccupation at once disciplinary and diverting. The Soviets appreciate the propaganda value of sports and hence its essential connection with the media—and, above all, with television—more intensely, more knowingly than any other government. They have achieved their greatest successes in international athletic competitions. On an aggregate of points the Soviets have "won" every Olympics, beginning with those held in Melbourne in 1956, only the second time they had participated in the games at all, having begun in 1952.

Athletics is the one field of endeavor in which the Soviets relentlessly pursue both quality and quantity. Their systems of talent scouting and training and their public sports programs involving a wide variety of disciplines (with, of course, special attention to Olympic disciplines) are as good as any in the world and far better than most. The Soviets also profit from a number of happy coincidences in the nature of things and their system, such as the affinities between collective spirit and team spirit, virtually unlimited funds within the scope of state sponsorship of all athletic activities, and the official elimination of the conceptual difference between the amateur and the professional athlete. (It would be hard to exaggerate the importance of this feat, which allows the Soviet Union to produce and cultivate professionals while ensuring their universal acceptance as amateurs. This is another prime example of the confusion of concepts and definitions.)

There is something more. In no arena of competition with the outside world in general do the Soviets apply such priorities as they do in athletics. There are few elite units in the Soviet Army, but the army of Soviet athletes in international competition is an elite force as a whole. Every Soviet athlete-competitor receives all the indoctrination and privileges (within a framework of strict discipline) of which the ideological caste system is capable. A victory is a matter of the highest national honor; a defeat is a national disgrace and hence a personal catastrophe for the vanquished. What witness of the finals in the 800-meter race in the 1972 Olympics in Munich can forget the spectacle of dejection presented by the Soviet runner Evgeny Arzhanov, who was overtaken ten yards before the finish line by the American (of all possible nationalities!) David Wottle. To add insult to injury, Wottle always ran with his hat on, a beaked, newsboy type of cap, an affront to the dignity of the Olympics and all its participants. During the ceremony in which he received the silver medal, Arzhanov looked as if he had been publicly apprehended betraying his country. It was a consummately pathological performance. But notwithstanding this and numerous similar scenes, the red flag continues to be raised and the Soviet national anthem struck up most often at the Olympic Games, wherever they take place.

In more recent Olympic times, Soviet teams have been pushed harder and harder by East German teams. Indeed, in the Winter Olympic Games in Sarajevo in early 1984 the East Germans outdid the Soviets, winning more gold medals and therefore a higher aggregate of points. Thus, when the Soviets announced their "irrevocable" decision in May 1984 not to participate in the Olympic Games at Los Angeles, the fear of risking a large number of defections ranked high among the various reasons attributed to the decision (not necessarily Soviet defections, it was pointed out; far more likely were fairly large-scale Polish defections at the games). Other reasons generally adduced were the Soviet fear of doing markedly less well this time than in the past—particularly against an American team performing on home ground as well as against the East Germans, who were especially strong in women's track and field events. It was also considered that the Soviets chose this means of underlining how seriously they regarded the existing international situation for which they inculpate the American government. Finally, most Europeans apparently felt that the Soviets were simply getting back at the Americans for boycotting the 1980 Olympic Games in Moscow: "Superpower see, superpower do."

Chapter II

Travelers to Saudi Arabia in the mid-sixties were astonished to find television sets in the middle of the desert, as it were, showing American television fare in the original (preeminently *I Love Lucy*), to the Bedouin—an exquisite anachronism involving perhaps 1,000 years, perhaps more. But in a sense all humanity is made up of Bedouin mesmerized by the television set as the operative element and chief symbol of modern media. Even New York, Parisian, or London audiences are hardly less prone—perhaps, indeed, more so—than their brethren in the Saudi desert to the psychological depredations of the electronic media.

It is axiomatic that scientific progress has outstripped progress in human affairs. It is surely less generally realized that technological developments in communications have overtaken and surprised the human, political animal effectively to a far greater extent than in any other scientific field. Certainly

Communists in general and Soviet Communists in particular are as alive as Americans to the overriding importance of the media. And in a significantly different way.

The fact is that scientific progress has played into the hands of the media commanders and panderers in a most ominous way.

It is literally impossible to exaggerate the actual, existent, in-being capacity for destruction of nuclear arms. It is now—already—technically possible to destroy not only humankind but virtually all forms of life on earth within a matter of minutes. The corollary of this fact—not a single flower left blooming in all the fields of the world—is hardly less dismaying. With the mere existence of the nuclear bomb and the intercontinental rocket, the armies of the world's overemotional and undereducated, the products of mass consumer, mass poverty, and mass media societies—East and West as well as North and South, under their commanders the psychopropagandists of the media and to the media—are at long last in possession of *the* incontrovertible argument: The apocalypse is upon us, up front and unmistakable.

Here is the quintessential confrontation—the encounter of Everyman point-blank with instantaneous annihilation. The hot-eyed, humorless bores of this world, whose chief pleasure in life is always being right—*Rechthaber* (the Germans have a world for it, as indeed they should)—have found the final, infallible formula: "Better red than dead." Who can argue with universal destruction? There is no joking about it, no humorous toying with the subject. It is absolute and overwhelming. With it the legions of the dim can scare hundreds of millions out of their wits, bring enormous pressures to bear on duly elected governments, and force major changes of policy.

This is to say that the central arena of the confrontation between the two superpowers is the media: press, radio, and television. The media are the center of the struggle because all issues and movements find their expression here and, contrariwise, many issues and movements are initiated in the media or come into being more or less inadvertently as a result of initiatives in the media.

Within the arena or, rather, the amphitheater of the electronic media—television in particular—the Soviets also benefit from general affinities between the nature of the mass media and the would-be massive monolithic nature of their system. Suffice it to cite Soviet "election" results, which invariably register absolute majorities of 98-plus percent. Television and radio lend themselves perfectly to the all-inclusively popular purpose of the Soviet system, the simple, wide-open, "square" message—the placard or billboard approach, about as subtle as a recruiting poster. *The* Soviet poet is Vladimir Mayakovsky, "the cloud in trousers" who wrote billboard poetry, stringing resounding slogans together.

The Soviet affinity with sloganeering from the very first is striking. Nadezhda Mandelstam vividly describes in her memoirs how astonished her husband, the poet Osip Mandelstam, was to receive from a government spokesman a slogan in answer to a penetrating question. "But that," sputtered Mandelstam, nonplussed, "is only a slogan!" Ah, yes—but *only* a slogan? Mandelstam made the same mistake on this occasion in 1920 as that of Richard Bernstein writing about the United Nations sixty-four years later in the *New York Times*: "Indeed, listening day after day to the speeches in the General Assembly or one of its seven committees, it is difficult to avoid the impression that the very notion of reasoned debate has fallen prey to a ritualistic and numbingly repetitive series of slogans that often constitute attacks, direct or implicit, on the United States." It is difficult to avoid the impression that the very notion of reasoned debate has fallen prey to the slogan because that is what in fact has happened.

Meanwhile, the Western allies and particularly the Americans have had some forty years' and more experience in dealing with the Soviets. The very length

of the period has provided hindsight and revealed a
number of the Soviets' favorite ploys. Perhaps the most
basic is the establishment of precedents in even the
smallest detail in procedure, protocol, and linguistic
usage. By this means the Soviets acquire tactical advantage in dealing with foreigners and, more important, set the framework for the redefinition of issues in
the Soviet sense. The mumbo jumbo of "a ritualistic
and numbingly repetitive series of slogans," as Bernstein puts it, always serves a distinct purpose.

If the Western allies benefit from hindsight, the Soviets profit all the more by the use of foresight. A striking example is their use of "out of band" broadcasting
wavelengths in the mid-thirties. These were, and are,
wavelengths not in the bands (scope) allocated for international broadcasting. Since this was before the bands
or wavelengths in general were assigned to anyone in
any great detail, the Soviets laid claim, as it were, by
using those not likely to be challenged in the immediate
or intermediate future and registering their usage with
the International Telecommunications Union (ITU).
Thus the Soviets stole a march by at least a decade on
the Americans, although not on the British (the BBC
was equally foresightful).

As it is, the Soviet Union floods the airwaves with
propaganda, broadcasting in 145 languages to the
United States' total of 75 and lavishly spending precious raw energy on the jamming of virtually all Western broadcasts. (The ratio of energy expenditure between
broadcasting and jamming is approximately one to four.)
By their painstaking and methodical preparatory
work in the field, the Soviets have put themselves
into an excellent position vis-à-vis all competitors for
the official allocation of wavelengths for shortwave
broadcasting within the World Administrative Radio
Conference (WARC).

The Soviets have always been acutely aware of both
the fact and the nature of the confrontation between
themselves and the United States. Writing in 1929,
Mayakovsky threw down the challenge in a poem entitled "Americans Are Surprised":

>   Bourgeois, be surprised at
>   the Communist side—
>   at work,
>   in the aeroplane,
>   in the car
>   your fleet-footed
>   famous America
>   we
>   shall catch up with
>   and overtake.

In 1983 Yuri Andropov laid it on the line: Our time, he said, "is marked by a confrontation, unprecedented in the entire postwar period, by its intensity and sharpness, between two diametrically opposed world outlooks, the two political courses of Socialism and Imperialism. A struggle is going on for the minds and hearts of billions of people on our planet." Fifty-five years after Mayakovsky threw down his challenge, the Americans are still surprised and just beginning to catch on.

During peacetime the public of a democracy keeps its eye on the budget. It was a restricted American budget that determined the NATO policy of massive retaliation ("a bigger bang for a buck!"), nuclear retaliation so massive that it lacked credibility. When NATO finally adopted the policy of flexible response in the sixties, it was more for show than for blow, the allies remaining at a two-to-one (at least) numerical disadvantage in manpower and conventional weapons vis-à-vis the Warsaw Pact.

The Soviets ultimately achieved something like nuclear parity in the seventies. At the advent of the eighties, having taken advantage of Jimmy Carter's cutback in military spending, the Soviets stole a nuclear march on the allies by installing medium-range rockets (some 600 of them at last count) along the western border of the Soviet Union and aimed at Western Europe. (The Americans had withdrawn their medium-range Atlas and Jupiter rockets from Turkey and Italy almost two decades earlier—unilaterally.) At this point the West Germans (Helmut Schmidt particularly) became restive and prevailed upon NATO to adopt the double-track decision, whereby the United States would install Pershing and cruise nuclear missiles to offset the Soviet missiles already installed—unless the Americans and the Soviets reached agreement in their pertinent disarmament negotiations in Geneva by late November 1983. The negotiations failed. Thus, undeterred by the massive propaganda and subversion efforts of the Soviet Union to foster and direct the homegrown anti-American peace movements in Western European countries, the Americans installed their rockets in Western Europe as prescribed by NATO.

The Soviets thereupon left all disarmament negotiations with the United States (two in Geneva and one in Vienna) and in retaliation installed more of their own medium-range rockets—but this time in Czechoslovakia and East Germany for good measure. Shortly thereafter a hack official Czech journalist wrote an article for the special Christmas supplement of a trade union daily in Prague warning all "honest and dishonest" foreign (which is to say, Western) diplomats in Czechoslovakia to beware of nuclear obliteration as they partook of their Christmas dinner. Since each side in the East–West confrontation scrutinizes the publications of the other as a matter of course, the article was picked up by Western wire services.

Thus from another direction—the financing of armaments via public approval—we come again to the main arena of the East–West, Soviet–American confrontation: the media. Each of the alliance systems is constrained by the nature of the struggle to address itself to the publics, rather than to the republics, of both its own and its adversary's constituencies. This condition, too, in terms of polity, is a deterioration.

Chapter III

The story of the confrontation between the Soviet Union and the United States of America is basically and in its beginning the story of the Greek East and the Latin West. It is a story almost as old as the story of the Christian Church itself.

Russia began to emerge as a state only after the sons of Rurik had seen Byzantium and after their sons' sons had accepted the Christian faith according to the Eastern rites. With the Christianization of both East and West, of course, came the civilizing and educational influence of the church. But there was a difference, beginning with that between Byzantium and Rome. The schism between the Eastern and Western churches was caused by the controversy over the indivisibility, as against the duality (and the son—*filioque*), of the Godhead. This, like the later difference over the nature and hierarchical situation of the bishops (the Greek idea of apostolic equality among bishops; the Latin idea of the preeminence of the bishop of Rome), found its counterpart in the differing conceptions of ecclesiastical organization and authority: the mystagogical, or spiritual, turning inward of the Greek Orthodox faith, as against the emphasis of the temporal mission of the priesthood of the Roman Catholic Church. These prefigured the withdrawn spirituality of the Russian Orthodox tradition in contrast with the dynamic involvement in wordly affairs characteristic of Catholicism and, to an even greater extent, of Protestantism (the lay minister in a business suit).

The basic traits of obedience and long-suffering passivity were embedded in the Russian psyche long before their association with the Eastern church. But it was a fateful coincidence and institutional reinforcement, the influence of which was as retarding for the Russians in terms of civic deportment as the Western church was a boon to the material and political prospering of its constituencies.

The Orthodox Church brought with it also the dream of empire, of world dominion. Particularly after the fall of Constantinople Moscow came to be regarded by many as the New Rome, the seat of a newer, purer ecumenicity. Indeed, there is a striking parallel between the transfer of the Holy Roman Empire to the German nation and the transfer of the Byzantine Empire ("the Second Rome") to the Russian nation. The idea of the Roman Empire as the universal and eternal ordering factor haunted the Germans until very recent times (Hitler was himself a distorted version of the Holy Roman Emperor of the German nation; much of his appeal to the German people was based on their instinctive appreciation of the greatest religious-political tradition the world has ever seen).

Likewise, for a great many Russians, Russia is not merely a state. It is a world, the true way (after the original Christian device which was "the way"). The Orthodox patriarch became the successor, in a sense, of the displaced Christian emperor, and the Russian nation inherited the *mission civilisatrice* of the Eastern Roman Empire to reshape the world. But the Orthodox version had this special feature: The world was to be

ARMAGEDDON IN PRIME TIME

reshaped in accordance with the spiritual values proclaimed and catechized by the Eastern church—ini-
tially *against* the materialism and secularism of the
West, later against the superficiality and tawdriness
of the bourgeoisie, and finally against the total phenomenon of Americanism.

This tradition has gone through several successive
stages as it has evolved through the centuries. It has
been consciously picked up, unconsciously assimilated,
inhaled in the air breathed by any number of Russian
writers, notably the Slavophiles—Dostoyevsky, Tol-
stoy, Leontiev, to name only the most prominent—and
by politicians and professional men as well. Generation
after generation the Russian spirit inherited the leg-
endary hatred of the West that was born in Byzantium.

Yet it was the church that provided by far the greater
part of lay instruction and general education in Russia.
In this sense it acted as the bridge between Greek East
and Latin West and brought to bear the humanizing
influences of both. And this did not change during the
radical secularization that occurred in the wake of the
Enlightenment in the early eighteenth century. When
Peter the Great introduced a new government policy,
it served, and was meant, to increase church involvement in education rather than to restrict religious
teaching per se. In his book *Russian Literature and
Ideology* Nicholas Rzhevsky points out that "even in a
secular society in which Orthodoxy was considered to
be but another administrative arm of the central authority, it was impossible to disregard the clergy's position as the social class with the most literate members.
Peter's famous tsifernye shkoly (cipher schools), through
which he hoped to develope [sic] the secular sciences of
mathematics and engineering, relied entirely on the
children of clergy for their student bodies." Rzhevsky
cites statistics compiled during the eighteenth and
nineteenth centuries to illustrate his point:

During the first half of the eighteenth century almost all books were of church origin; in the second
half—with secularization in full swing—out of 8,000

39

texts printed, 60 per cent were still totally religious in content. At the middle of the following century (1855) out of 19,060 educational institutions counted in the census, more than 70 per cent (13,600) turned out to be parish schools. With the twentieth century seven years away, new statistics show that the various zemstvoes and ministries together list 25,978 schools and are almost equally matched by the parishes (25,501).

Religion, like anything else but more than anything else, is a matter of communication. The special science of religious communication—that is to say, the interpretation of Scripture—is called hermeneutics (after Hermes, the messenger of the gods).

In the beginnings of Western civilization, both Greek East and Latin West, religion and mythology (which is pagan religion) were the backbone of literature; the Greek philosophers cited the works of Homer as though they were Scripture. Indeed, literature, like hermeneutics, is interpretation in the broadest sense: the interpretation of life by the assignment of significances and the setting of values, or not (which, within the literary framework, comes to the same thing). One can be an inheritor of a tradition and be in rebellion against the tradition. Indeed, one can be all the more an inheritor for being in rebellion.

Dostoyevsky is a case in point; it is very easy to demonstrate the influence of the Russian Orthodox faith and even its strict doctrinal instruction on him. But it is something else to explain, let alone trace, how he solved the most difficult of all literary problems—namely the effective presentation of the positive hero, the promotion, in artistic form, of the good man. Dostoyevsky turned the tables on the literary tradition he inherited. The "superfluous man," the negative hero so popular in nineteeth-century Russian literature, in his hands became a truly tragic figure, the godless man suffering the consequences of his godlessness at every turn.

Dostoyevsky's works, the great novels foremost

among them, probably constitute the most significant corpus of lay religious writing in the whole of human history. His characters—Myshkin, Raskolnikov, the brothers Karamazov, Stravrogin, the Underground Man—dominate Russian literary and political consciousness (of course, their domination does not stop with the Russians) as do no others.

Dostoyevsky set the course of both Russian and Western spiritual evaluation unalterably in a direction that has foiled all collective attempts to create a literary or other aesthetic counterforce. He blocked the routes of access to Communist or pronouncedly socialist intellectual development. In *The Possessed* Dostoyevsky foresaw the coming of communism and predicted its nature and its attributes. He presented—half a century before its actual emergence—the whole typology of communism, describing the kinds of men who imposed the system and the traits of character that made them what they were: jailers.

A Day in the Life of Ivan Denisovich was published in 1963 as the result of a most un-Soviet lapsus in the course of Khrushchev's de-Stalinization campaign. The lapsus was unique and short.

When Andrey Sinyavsky and Yuri Daniel (writing under the pseudonyms of Abram Tertz and N. Arzhak) were arrested in 1964, the official newspaper of the Soviet state accused them of treason. Their writings were described by Soviet authorities as "ideological espionage." There was logic in the use of this term. In the Soviet Union's totally ideological society, the writer is a key figure, the "engineer of the human soul" as Stalin called him, the exemplary disciple of *partiinost'* ("party spirit"), which is the demiurge that creates or abolishes facts, that confers existence and significance on men or events or else annuls them, for the writer is the interpreter of history in the making or remaking—past, present, and future.

To bind the writer to the party cause, the theory of socialist realism was propounded in 1934 at the first congress of the Soviet Writers' Union, which included in its statutes: "Socialist realism, which constitutes the

41

basic method of Soviet artistic literature and literary criticism, demands from the artist a truthful, historico-concrete representation of reality in its revolutionary development." Karl Radek, in his rejection of the realism practiced by James Joyce in *Ulysses* (Joyce was too impartial: "We should select...all phenomena which show how the system of capitalism is being smashed, how socialism is growing..."), made it clear at the congress that socialist realism was the groundwork for a dogma that would reduce the function of literature to the illustration and eulogy of party decisions.

To secure the primacy of "party spirit" in Soviet letters, a permanent ideological emergency was proclaimed in the mid-twenties and has been periodically reproclaimed since then. A state of acute revolutionary urgency was simulated and made the statutory foundation of Soviet society. For this reason, any information reflecting Soviet policy or from which Soviet policy is even vaguely deducible became, and remains, the object of obsessive secrecy. This applies, above all, to statistics and, by extension, to any form of inquiry potentially contributory to the compilation of data. The end result of this combination of developments is the complicated, grotesque, and scarcely sufferable situation concealed under the cliché "closed society."

A specific result has been the repression of Soviet journalism and much of Soviet creative writing to the level of advertising. Most Soviet journalists and creative writers are in effect admen, hucksters whose blurbs are designed to popularize the party-state. The great bulk of actual reportage in the Soviet system by Soviet writers is in the field of belles lettres and particularly in poetry, since the author must mask his findings in literary forms, parables, allegories, or systems of metaphor. If he wishes to report the Soviet scene straight, he is bound to go outside the system. Thus by definition he commits an anti-Soviet act, and the least he may expect is to be pilloried by some loyal party critic for having produced "a vicious caricature of our reality."

Such efforts inevitably lead to a literature of subversion, to underground literature and a literary underground. The result was the appearance of the phenomenon *samizdat*: bootleg literature. Many of the most distinguished Soviet writers entered the world of samizdat, where it is only a matter of time (usually a short time) before copies are smuggled out to the West and published there.

In his activity as a literary critic writing in the monthly journal *New World*, Andrey Sinyavsky came to the special notice of Soviet readers in early 1960, when he drew heavy fire from no fewer than six party hack writers because of an article in which he and a coauthor examined the published verses of a young woodcutter and concluded that the author was a woodcutter, not a poet. The burden of the rebuttals was that the woodcutter might perhaps not be a first-class poet (although this was doubtful), but he was a first-class woodcutter, and that was what really counted. The six hacks shared the conviction that the disparagement of the author's ability as a poet reflected on his skill and dignity as a woodcutter.

In their reply the two critics were reduced to putting a rhetorical question that was well over forty years old at the time: Is it possible for a good worker to write bad verses? For this was reminiscent of the early twenties' polemics during the cult of the proletariat, according to which the workers—if given an opportunity and the necessary orders and quotas—would surely be able to turn out masterpieces worthy of Homer, Shakespeare, and Pushkin, at least on a percentage basis. (The proletcult method of literary production was described by Lenin as one in which "ten hysterical maidens keep blowing at one budding worker-author until they have extinguished every spark of talent in him.")

The cult of the proletariat was replaced subsequently but not entirely by the cult of personality. The purpose of the policy of de-Stalinization was to validate the party's contention that the cult of personality was chiefly, if not entirely, the fault of Stalin. The immediate aim of the Soviet literary underground in general was to demonstrate that the cult of personality was inherent in the system.

In Sinyavsky's first clandestine work, the critical analysis entitled "What Is Socialist Realism?", which served as a sort of floor plan for his and Daniel's subsequent clandestine production, he shows that at the basis of the formula for socialist realism is the concept of the goal, of the all-embracing ideal, in the direction of which, unerringly and "revolutionarily," reality is developing. To spotlight the movement toward the goal and to promote the approach to the goal by remaking the consciousness of the reader and orienting him toward the goal is the function of socialist realism. "The goal," writes Sinyavsky, "is Communism.... The poet does not simply write verses, but helps the construction of Communism with his verses. This is just as natural as it is for the sculptor, the musician, the agronomist, the engineer, the manual laborer, the militiamen, the lawyer and others to make the same contribution at his side."

The lumping together of the whole range of honorable human activities under the heading of "Contributions to Communism" is in large part responsible for the continual side-door entry of the cult of the proletariat. Because of the imperative need to transmute the value of labor experience into poetic values, the function of the poet must be to certify the activities of all other worker contributors to communism. This has led a number of workers—both skilled and unskilled—to mistake job description for literary production, avowedly in the belief that if the worker eulogizes his work in verse, he is of necessity a poet. The result has been insuperable confusion.

Unfortunately, Sinyavsky points out, the Soviet writer's nearest available model is the hero in nineteenth-century Russian literature, the unsocial "superfluous man," the brilliant but inwardly sick hero, such as Pushkin's Eugene Onegin, and Chekhov's gallery of bumbling characters in search of themselves who never knew what they wanted until it was too late and in no case could get it. They all were decadents, dreamers, dandies, or demons, "lamentable examples no good to anyone," least of all to themselves—the diametric opposite of communism's "positive hero," who has no doubt about what he wants, is never slowed down by the slightest indecision, can solve any problem quickly and easily, has none but the most negligible vices. He is "an iron man in a leather coat," like Commissar Davidov in Mikhail Sholokhov's novel *Virgin Soil Upturned*, which would have been more fittingly entitled "The Importance of Being Sternest."

The trouble, writes Sinyavsky, is that Soviet writers know all there is to know about the superfluous man and the great masters who created him: "We all want to become famous and write like Chekhov. From this duality monsters were born. It is impossible to create a 'positive hero' and equip him with human psychology. In trying to do both we have succeeded in doing neither." The Communist writers, while concentrating on the conscious element in human behavior, neglected or at least failed to devise a method to remake or control the subconscious.

Admittedly two Soviet writers succeeded—but only two. They have remained exceptions. As noted, the poet Mayakovsky, who committed suicide in 1930, made a clean break with the past and worked straight to revolutionary purpose, painting figures as big and as simple as billboards. Sholokhov, in *And Quiet Flows the Don*, produced a revolutionary period piece at once acceptable to the party and widely acclaimed. He won the Nobel Prize in literature in 1965. But the real need of socialist realism is for a religious art "of pure invention and fantasy within agreed forms." At the bottom of it all, "Socialist realism is a contradiction in terms," for it tries to depict not what is but what should be. According to Sinyavsky's analysis, socialist realism has corrupted the very concept of reality in Soviet society. Declaring representation of reality to be wholly subject to activist, "goal-oriented" interpretation created an enormous administrative and disciplinary problem and accordingly magnified the need for bureaucratic manipulation at every level of intellectual pursuit.

For this reason Stalin dabbled in linguistic theory, and Khrushchev delivered a 15,000-word address to the assembled artists and writers of the Soviet Union, laying down guidelines for each department ("in music we like a simple melody..."). In the event the theory became hopelessly confused with the principle it was designed to apply. The principle of party spirit—the complete identification of the individual with the collective—had to be invoked at every turn in applying the theory. The result was an administrative invasion of privacy on a scale and with an intensity unprecedented in history and, in the wake of the invasion, a confusion of definitions and standards that has redoubled the need for interpretation. The wheel comes full circle viciously.

The only way out, concludes Sinyavsky, is "to drop the concern for realism and concentrate on presenting the sublime unreality of our epoch." This was the task Sinyavsky and Daniel set themselves in their clandestine literary production, in which they took recourse to the fantastic, the ribald, and the absurd in order to expose the phantasmagoria of Soviet life. In Sinyavsky's *The Trial Begins*, the system is allegorized in the character of an impotent adulterer. Daniel's "This is Moscow Speaking" describes the consequences of the Soviet government's declaring "a day of open and legalized murder" after the fashion of the Soviet "Day of the Teacher," "Day of the Miner," etc.

"In Sinyavsky-Tertz's libelous story 'Lyubimov,'" said *Izvestia* on January 13, 1966, "the author's purpose is no more and no less than to show that the very idea of Communist reconstruction of society is an unattainable illusion.... Its conceptual political core is completely clear: it is an unbridled mockery of the laws of history, of those who gave their lives in battle for our great goals; it is mockery of the country and people. Here the insolence of the author attains truly Homeric proportions... to what heights of philistine sadism does he not rise, showing the ruination of the city of Lyubimov, in which a certain Tikomirov contrives to achieve general happiness by practicing mass hypnotism." The hypnotist has the citizenry believing that mineral water is vodka, that the river flows with champagne, and that red peppers are Polish sausages. "With what gusto does Sinyavsky describe the fiasco that follows the Communist experiment and the return of the citizens of Lyubimov to the old order of life."

Understandably, *Izvestia* did not mention then, and has not mentioned since, Daniel's short story "Redemption."

This work describes the plight of a man falsely accused of denouncing a friend to the police. In the nature of things he cannot prove his innocence and is ostracized. Even his fiancée leaves. Though she does not believe in his guilt, she cannot stand the ordeal of his ostracism. In the end the hero comes to the conclusion that he bears responsibility (along with all Soviet citizens) for his denunciation because he has tolerated a system that turns on denunciation.

For five years Sinyavsky and Daniel availed themselves of a "pipeline" running from Moscow to Paris courtesy of the French diplomatic pouch (Helène Zamoyska-Pelletier—the daughter of the French naval attaché in Moscow—was a fellow student at the University of Moscow). Only by use of pseudonyms could the two writers have managed to produce a corpus of clandestine work. But the fact that each used only one pseudonym was to have consequences for both writers.

It is against this background that the case of Sinyavsky and Daniel assumes its true significance. A literary underground of sorts had always existed in the Soviet Union (Mandelstam's poem about Stalin that made the rounds of Moscow and Leningrad from pocket to pocket probably signed the poet's death warrant). Poems, short stories, and even novels had been copied by hand and on typewriters and passed along until the paper disintegrated. As early as 1959 underground groups began printing "magazines" of two, three, and four pages on hand presses and makeshift duplicating machines. They steadily increased in variety, bulk, and circulation. Their titles were significant: *Boomerang* (1959–1960), *Phoenix* (1961), *Lantern* (1963), *Workshop, Leningrad* (1964), *Sphinx, Avant-Garde, South Smog, Ural Smog, Smog Youth, Neck, Kolokol* (1965).

The *Kolokol* Group (*Kolokol*, or *Bell*, was the title of
Aleksandr Herzen's famous Russian-language émigré
newspaper) when discovered and arrested in 1965 turned
out to be a number of graduate chemistry students at
the University of Leningrad. These publications rarely
survived two issues. A good many of the editors and
contributors—especially those responsible for earlier
publications—were arrested and given lengthy prison
sentences—and the small groups continually had to
change the locale of their operations and begin anew.

In retaliation the students and writers concerned
formed an illegal coordinating organization under the
name the Avant-Garde of Russian Art. When it publicized itself by sponsoring a number of clandestine publications in 1965, the Moscow literary newspaper
Literaturnaya Gazeta ridiculed the organization, dub-
bing it the Most Powerful Society of Geniuses (SMOG).
The members of the underground accepted the title with
delight and went on to use it on various of their publications.

Far more important than the spread of clandestine
printing, however, has been the mass sale of tape recorders. This has gone hand in hand with the great
popularity of bootleg recordings of poems, songs, and
stories. The most popular genre of underground literature—that dealing with Soviet concentration camps—
gained currency in this way. In this way, too, the Geor-
gian-Armenian poet Bulat Akhudzhava, the chief ex-
ponent of concentration camp songs, became the most
popular balladeer in the Soviet Union. Yet Akhudzhava
has never made a record (there is as yet no underground
recording factory) and has never sung on the radio (although he is allowed to make public appearances). The
late Aleksandr Galich (who died in 1977), certainly the
balladeer second only to Akhudzhava in the Soviet
Union, had likewise never cut a record, never sung on
the radio. And unlike Akhudzhava, he had never once
made a public appearance as a singer, yet his voice was
known and loved throughout the Soviet Union, thanks
only to *magnitizdat* (the electronic equivalent of samizdat). However, a number of records of Akhudzhava's

. and Galich's songs have been cut and placed on sale in the West. Galich spent the last three years of his life in exile in Western Europe, and Akhudzhava has spent more than one long vacation in Paris.

The electronic aspect of the technical revolution, specifically broadcasts beamed to the Soviet Union by the Voice of America, Radio Liberty, the BBC, and other Western stations, broke the Soviets' mass communications monopoly from outside, while the mass consumer revolution that put tape recorders on the Soviet market at reasonable prices broke the government's literary monopoly from the inside. As a result, beginning in the late fifties, for the first time in Soviet history there has been a public opinion at least partly free from direct administrative control. To accommodate this development in the hope of containing it, the Soviet authorities have made procedural and policy adjustments in literature (including journalism) and the arts.

It was this defensive tactic that made Yevgeny Yevtushenko the swearing parrot of the Soviet regime. Similarly, *Literaturnaya Gazeta (Literary Gazette)*, in 1,545 lines of print, published a rejection of *Doctor Zhivago* that had been sent to Boris Pasternak by the magazine *Novy Mir (New World)* and which contained several passages from the novel selected to document its revisionist and anti-Soviet character. The issue was sold out within three hours. The publications of the *Zhivago* excerpts was a provocation, but one that was presented and accepted as a necessary evil, making it possible for officials to say that parts of the novel had been published and justice done. The fact that the excerpts selected for condemnation were precisely those which the public was most interested in reading was perhaps simply the purpose of the exercise.

In any case *Novy Mir* had already come to be regarded as the leader of the liberal attack against the bastion of socialist realism. The double edge of accommodative containment is serviceable to both the opposition and the regime. It was in *Novy Mir* in 1963 that there occurred a literary event, one that burst like a comet on the Soviet horizon and remained there as a fixed star: the publication of Solzhenitsyn's *A Day in the Life of Ivan Denisovich*. This was a perfectly astonishing development as the result of a peculiar constellation of political and literary factors: Khrushchev's need for a clincher in his anti-Stalin campaign, the character and literary devotion of *Novy Mir*'s editor, Aleksandr Tvardovsky, and the extraordinary acumen of Solzhenitsyn himself. For a time thereafter the dissidents (as they came to be called) actually dreamed of taking over *Novy Mir* as their citadel in the Soviet battleground of the media and the arts. The dream was short.

Instead, the dissident writers, artists, and students were deported (like Solzhenitsyn and later Vladimir Bukovsky), given the choice of going East—Siberia—or West (like Vladimir Maximov, Sinyavsky, Andrey Amalric, Viktor Nekrassov, among many others), or hounded by the police and official thugs until they "voluntarily" applied for permission to leave the country (Vladimir Voinovich, Georgi Vladimov). The body politic of the Soviet Union shed its foremost artists and writers like so much waste, a process that prompted Solzhenitsyn, in his monumental *The Gulag Archipelago*, to compare the Soviet penal system and its network of concentration camps and prisons to a giant sewage system. The result is that the best of the Soviet Union's writers and many of its best artists—directors, choreographers, dancers, musicians, and journalists—are now permanently outside the country in permanent enforced or voluntary exile. Politically, Soviet society is the purest society in the world, and the most sterile.

Chapter IV

In 1964 I was taken by car on a regular tour from Moscow to Zagorsk, the Russian Orthodox "Vatican" and the site of some thirty-six churches of varying degrees of magnificence. My Intourist guide was a young man, perhaps in his mid-thirties. We spoke Russian.

"Have you read *Doctor Zhivago*?" he asked. I said I had.

"How did you like it?"

"So-so," I said. I was tired, and I did not want to start an ideological argument.

"Well, *I* thought it was brilliant!" he said.

"Now that you mention it, so did I," I said, "but tell me, how did you manage to get hold of it?"

"Oh, well, of course I read it in English translation," he said.

I paused and looked out the window. Then I said, "How does that strike you? You, the Russian, you read a work which belongs in the mainstream of

51

Russian literary tradition in an English translation smuggled into your country, while I, the foreigner, the American, *I* read the work in the Russian original smuggled out of your country! How does that strike you?"

He did not answer. Nor did we speak so much as another word to each other during the long day's journey.

It is not too much to say that the debate about the nature and the affairs of the Soviet Union, as a result of the largely successful suppression and deportation of the dissidents, has shifted from the Soviet Union itself to the West, where it by and large swirls around the figure and position of Aleksandr Solzhenitsyn. Solzhenitsyn's "moral-absolutist" position on world affairs (the term does not do justice to Solzhenitsyn's position) and his Slavophile proclivities tend to polarize the Soviet democratic movement, it is said. It is certainly true that the self-styled democrats of the movement, which is by and large synonymous with its liberal left wing, are frequently more upset over the statements and speeches of Solzhenitsyn (the Harvard speech, the Taiwan speech) than over the actions and statements of the Soviet regime. Andrei Sakharov has called Solzhenitsyn "a giant in the struggle for human dignity," and indeed, he strides the two worlds of communism and free enterprise like a colossus.

Not that other émigrés do not have and maintain their contacts within the Soviet Union; many if not most dissidents in exile have their relatives, friends, and followers in their home country and manage somehow to correspond with them. But Solzhenitsyn is of another magnitude; he is a major societal force in himself.

It is he, and only he, who, in the words of the late Andrey Amalric, "is toasted every night by at least thirty members of the Central Committee of the Communist Party of the Soviet Union." There is a movement (however slight) on the part of some Soviet officials—

diplomats and functionaries having something to do with foreign affairs—to encourage or discourage various dissidents in specific instances ("Tell the boys [a dissident group in Paris]," said a Soviet ambassador to a NATO country, "to keep up the good work.") Yes, or to "cool it," as the case may be. It is as if the factions within the Soviet establishment (not just the party), which are something like embryonic parties in themselves, carried out their struggles not within the Soviet Union (where no public expression is possible) but in the emigration by proxy by designated or voluntary (and sometimes unwelcome) representatives.

Unfortunately the KGB and the GRU (Soviet military intelligence) play the same game from better positions and so compromise the entire phenomenon to a large extent.

But there is only one Solzhenitsyn fund. In 1974, almost immediately after he had been forcibly flown out of the Soviet Union, Solzhenitsyn created the Russian Social Fund for the Persecuted and Their Families in the USSR and arranged to have it financed from the royalties accruing from *The Gulag Archipelago.* The arrangement is comprehensive: All royalties from the work go to the fund. From mid-1974 on, the fund has helped many thousands of political prisoners and their families. When General Pyotr Grigorenko was finally released from prison, he was contacted by the director of the fund and enabled to survive until he was given an exit visa by the Soviet authorities.

The directors of the fund, beginning with Aleksandr Ginzburg, have been hounded and beaten up by the police, arrested, imprisoned, and sent West to freedom in exile or East to Siberia. It is an altogether extraordinary operation run by altogether extraordinary people. The money goes to keep the families of political prisoners alive and more or less healthy and to enable mothers, wives, or children to visit the imprisoned family member whenever authorized. (Since great distances are frequently involved, such visits would then otherwise be impossible.)

Some of the fund's former directors (Ginzburg, Kronid Liubarsky, Georgi Davidov) have been in the West now for several years. Through friends and acquaintances they are in more or less substantive contact with the present fund's director (de facto, if not de jure—as already mentioned, fund directors spend a good deal of time in custody) and even manage to field questionnaires to the fund's clients through the directors or their assistants on their treatment in prison, the identities, and personalia of the culprits concerned in cases of mishandling, etc. The fact that one of these questionnaires was found among the papers of a fund director during a KGB search of his living quarters in 1982 led to his being charged with high treason rather than with the usual Paragraph 58 (anti-Soviet activity). The charge of high treason carries with it the statutory (but not mandatory) death penalty.

This development posed a nice dilemma: Does the director of the Solzhenitsyn fund have the right to combine his function with the gathering of information on prison conditions, including the personalia of the guards? When the guards are military men, as they often are, the implication of espionage is given. If one accepts the exclusive preference of the primary function of the fund, one admits therewith the ability of the Soviets to impose their interpretation on the circumstances surrounding the phenomenon of gulag. This is an acceptance that a good many people concerned are not willing to make.

In the mid-seventies I had access to a publisher's report concerning the sales to that date in hardback of the twelve volumes that made up the works of Aleksandr Solzhenitsyn. One total was for the German-speaking area (deutschsprachiger Raum); the other was for the French-speaking area (territoire de la langue française). For the German speaking area the total—I repeat, in hardback—was 14 million plus. For the French-speaking (les regions Francophones) area the total was 7 million plus. As a rule of thumb one can posit a minimum of 10 percent of the store sale price to the author and an average store sale price of $10. I cannot remember what the breakdown of the sales figures was book by book. I do remember that the sales figures for *The Gulag Archipelago* were by far the largest.

Chapter V

There is no more instructive example of Soviet information brokerage than the case of Andrei Sakharov. Almost certainly the most prestigious Soviet scientist alive, "the father of the Soviet hydrogen bomb," three-time recipient of the Order of Lenin and a host of other awards, Sakharov gradually moved in his public statements from a position more or less in line with, or at least not openly contradictory to, official Soviet propaganda to a position of outright, categorical, and condemnatory opposition to the Soviet system itself.

As long as Sakharov more or less supported official Soviet foreign policy—particularly in his sometime representation of China as the main external threat to the country—he was permitted to live and work largely unharassed by the security organs of the state.

Solzhenitsyn, for his part, continues to regard China as the main external danger to the Soviet Union; this concern prompted him to travel to Taiwan and make a major, supportive speech there. These are events that throw some light on the Soviet dilemma vis-à-vis China altogether.

But when Sakharov changed his position on China, ceased to consider himself a "socialist," and announced himself a liberal, proceeding to insist that everything— détente, survival, progress, et al.—depended on the abolition of the KGB and the establishment of the full panoply of conventional democratic rights and procedures, he was quickly subjected to the entire claviature of Soviet repressive measures, including exile in Gorky, a city that is off limits to foreigners, and excepting only—to date—incarceration in a concentration camp and commitment to a psychiatric clinic.

In all probability he has been spared outright incarceration only because of his prestige in major Western countries and in the international scientific community. He has received any number of official invitations of greater or lesser duration from various Western institutions and even governments.

In 1983 President Reagan proclaimed a "Sakharov Day." The same year saw the foundation of a Sakharov Institute in the United States. Various combinations of members of national scientific academies have signed petitions to various purposes in favor of Sakharov, his wife Yelena G. Bonner, and their families.

The Soviets, for their part, have succeeded in all but isolating Sakharov from the outside world. As a result of this isolation, the controversies of the Soviet emigration have taken directions often far afield from their areas of relevancy. This is particularly true of the so-called great debate between Sakharov and Solzhenitsyn. Sakharov has made his way through various stages, to a position of what can be called liberal humanism. He has arrived at the conclusion that the only hope for the Soviet Union (and perhaps for the world altogether) is the introduction of all the conventional Western democratic freedoms as soon as possible—particularly freedom of information.

Solzhenitsyn, who is a profoundly religious man, a moral philosopher, is suspicious of many Western "values" and the humanistic idea of linear technological progress. He questions whether the Soviet Union, once freed from the Communist yoke, would be ready for full-blown democracy Western-style and recommends instead the establishment of a transitional authoritarian system, albeit with the basic democratic freedoms guaranteed. In his reply to Sakharov's answer to his "Letter to the (Soviet) Leaders," an impassioned plea to forswear imperial designs and concentrate on the needs of the Russian nation, a sort of "small is beautiful" approach, Solzhenitsyn wrote: "I am happy to note that the number of questions he and I are in agreement about today is incomparably greater than it was six years ago, when we became acquainted.... (I should like to hope that in another six years the area of our agreement will double.)" Sakharov's increasing isolation at the hands of the Soviet authorities, culminating in his being exiled to Gorky, put the quietus on any such hope.

Now all the big names are in the West—save two: Yevgeny Yevtushenko, while dissenting, was never a dissident and has managed to keep his privileges (in an interview with an Italian magazine two years ago he stated that he simply lacked the courage to be a dissident); Yuri Daniel preferred to remain in the Soviet Union because he wanted to be near his son. But what a glittering roster it is: Solzhenitsyn, Andrey Sinyavsky, Vladimir Bukovsky, Mstislav Rostropovich, Shostakovich (son and grandson of the composer), Svetlana Alliluyeva, Vladimir Maximov, Valevy Chalidze, Eduard Kuznetsov, Aleksandr Shimyakin, Mikhail Baryshnikov, Aleksandr Godunov, Oleg Bitov, Georgi Lyubimov, Viktor Nekrassov, Aleksandr Ginsburg, Joseph Brodsky, Ernst Neizvestny, Georgi Vladimov, Vladimir Voinovich, Natalia Gorbanyevskaya.... The cream of the Soviet cultural crop is in the West. And Soviet cultural policy is in a shambles.

Perhaps the pithiest description of the Soviet cultural bureaucracy was given by Yuri Lyubimov in London just after he had been relieved of his post as director of the famous Taganka Theater in Moscow and then deprived of his Soviet citizenship: "They have thrown me out of the theater I created. They have taken away the most precious thing I had—the chance to carry on with twenty years' work. How dare they? No foreign enemy, no matter how much he hated Russia, could possibly do the damage to our culture that these stupid little men have done."

What caused the ruckus with Lyubimov in the first place is then revealed. Three of his productions were banned consecutively. One of them, Pushkin's *Boris Godunov*, has a scene in which a boyar reproaches the Russian crowd for doing nothing against tyranny: "Why do you remain silent?" In Lyubimov's version the actor playing the boyar goes down into the audience at the final curtain (he is out of costume) and asks the same question. The Soviet cultural bureaucracy has its work cut out. But it still manages to hold the line. And keep the Soviet Union largely incommunicado.

The fact is that the Soviet Union regards information in general as the most sensitive form of matter in existence, more explosive than nuclear bombs because it is so much more difficult to control. Soviet authorities take infinite pains with the gathering, evaluating, preparation, and dissemination of it.

Before even an ordinary news item appears in print in the Soviet Union, it goes through some ten stages of control. The Soviets have an almost mystic sense of awe in the presence of the printed or broadcast word. This accounts in good part for the curious chronic shortage of printed matter, even of speech and narrative on Soviet radio and television. This pervasive censorship has created a situation in which anything that appears in print or is broadcast must be accepted as enjoying official sanction. Indeed, printed matter takes on something of the nature of legal tender.

This situation explains the extraordinary impact of samizdat on the Soviet public. Samizdat represents nothing less than the private usurpation of the government's arrogated right to manufacture and control information. This, in turn, points up the dilemma of the

Soviet authorities in dealing with the dissidents who must be prosecuted much as if they were counterfeiters. The dissident cannot be allowed to stay in the Soviet Union once he or she has become established as a samizdat author. The dissident's continued presence on Soviet soil would imply a sort of passive official sanction. The toleration of the established dissident by the Soviet authorities would thus in itself tend to legalize the opposition.

Consider how infinitely sparing of personal publicity the Soviet Union is. Little, if anything, is ever said of the private life and little enough of the public life of even the most prominent or highly placed Soviet officials. To repeat an observation made earlier: Any information reflecting Soviet policy or from which Soviet policy is even vaguely deducible became, and remains, the object of obsessive secrecy.

I once asked the Soviet ambassador in West Germany what had happened to the famous World War II Soviet ace Aleksandr Pokrishkin, three times winner of the highest Soviet medal for bravery, the gold star of a "Hero of the Soviet Union." (I remembered hearing German pilots during the war on shortwave radio: *"Achtung! Achtung!* Pokrishkin is airborne!") "Presumably," answered the ambassador with visible irritation, "he is somewhere in the air force." Presumably he was.

But it is not extraordinary—it is merely typical—how much of life in the Soviet Union is shrouded in secrecy. The confrontation of the totalitarian state with the phenomenon of privacy, of the privacy of its citizens puts the state automatically into the position of a tiny minority—albeit at the apex of the political power structure—and renders government leadership a clique that is forced to shroud itself in secrecy in order to maintain control of the people.

To maintain control, the totalitarian state must resort to terror, whether in the extreme form of arbitrary

GEORGE BAILEY

arrest and execution with or without a show trial or in
the milder form of arbitrary administrative coercion.
As a later vintage proverb has it, "Those who identify
with the Soviet system are conventional criminals and
those who keep their distance from it are political 'criminals.'" The criminalization of politics is the donnée of
the totalitarian state. The Soviet state, according to the
dissident Vladimir Telnikov, is a criminal institution.

This accounts in no small way for the striking sim-
ilarity between the secretive totalitarian state and the
clandestine terrorist groups that arrogate the status
and function of a government in imposing death "sentences" and carrying out "executions," demanding official recognition while their effectiveness and indeed
their very existence depend on their continuing clandestinity. The secretiveness of the totalitarian state is
the main reason for its extreme sensitivity to "outside
interference in internal affairs"; anything that does not
originate within the clique is by definition "outside interference." It is also the reason for the Soviet Union's
perennial quest for legitimacy.

This is government in ambush, a system which Adolf
Hitler described succinctly: "As few as possible to know
as little as possible as late as possible." In a totalitarian
regime the public domain is strictly the province of the
state. The ownership of the means of production very
much includes the means of production of ideas and
opinions and their dissemination. The Soviets adhere
as strictly as they can to Lenin's concept of socialist
realism: "not what is, but what should be."

The trouble with this philosophy is that ideas of "what
should be" change as tactical considerations change.
The Soviet establishment's contempt for facts as such
has gradually become notorious. In an article in the
dissident quarterly magazine *Kontinent* entitled "The
Seven Deaths of Maxim Gorky" the Polish exile writer
Gustav Herling-Grudzinski has listed the six different
official Soviet versions of the writer's death and docu-
mented a seventh on the basis of his own findings. The
first version, published shortly after Gorky's death,

stated that the "literary genius and unselfish friend of
the working class" had died of pneumonia. In version
number two, published in 1938, the chief of the NKVD,
G. G. Yagoda, confessed that he had murdered Gorky.
In version number three Stalin's secretary Aleksandr
Poskribyshev, in his contribution to an anthology dated
1940, denied the first version of Gorky's death. A *Pravda*
commentary in 1951 stated that Gorky "and others"
had been poisoned by foreign intelligence agencies; this
was the fourth version. In the same year, the fifteenth
anniversary of Gorky's death, a series of commemora-
tive publications did not so much as hint that anything
untoward had happened to him; this, the fifth version,
was thus a corroboration of the first version. But according to the *Great Soviet Encyclopedia* of 1952, Gorky
was murdered by "enemies of the people belonging to
a rightist-Trotzkist organization"; this was version
number six. Finally Herling-Grudzinski unearthed a
report of one of Gorky's doctors who affirmed that Gorky
and two male nurses had been poisoned by means of a
gift box of chocolates: number seven.

The *Great Soviet Encyclopedia*, in its succeeding edi-
tions, is the chief repository of varying versions of events,
particularly recent events. The Yugoslav harbor town
of Zadar, for example, is described as "an Anglo-Amer-
ican imperialist base" because the encyclopedia was
published in 1952, not long after the Soviet Union's
break with Marshal Tito's government. In Volume T,
however (published in 1956—that is, after the Soviet-
Yugoslav reconciliation), Tito is described as "the most
outstanding Yugoslav leader, tireless champion of the
working classes," etc. An unsuspecting reader could assume from the two items that part of the country, at
least the Dalmatian coast, was somehow under Western
allied occupation.

The vagaries of the fifty-five-volume *Great Soviet
Encyclopedia* are so many that they would fill the pages
of a fifty-five-volume encyclopedia. The reader of Volume K searches in vain for Franz Kafka and finds instead Vladimir Kafka, a sculptor—to be sure, a Czech

sculptor. The most significant episode in the history of the *Great Soviet Encyclopedia* remains that day in 1953 when each subscriber received a razor blade through the mail along with instructions to cut out the two pages on Lavrenti Beria, who had just been liquidated, and replace them with enclosed pages on the Bering Strait.

Chapter VI

There are, at the present, two great nations, Russia and the US which...started from different points but which seem to tend toward the same end...the American struggles against the obstacles that nature opposes to him....the adversaries of the Russian are men. The former combats the wilderness...the latter, civilizations. The principal of the former is freedom, of the latter servitude. Yet each seems called by some secret design of providence one day to hold in its hands the destinies of half the world.

So wrote Alexis de Tocqueville in his masterpiece on the American nation. Even at the beginning of the eighteenth century the confrontation of the two nations was clearly in the making. Equally clear are the creation and development of the American nation as an expression of the unfolding of the religious faith and tradition of the Latin West. The discovery and gradual imposition of America on European consciousness coincided with the Reformation and the Counterreformation and the tremendous forces the two movements released.

From the very first the huge, unknown continent shimmered in the Western European's imagination as the "promised land," as safe haven for the oppressed and particularly for the religiously oppressed. The idea of freedom, which is inseparably associated with the very name America, was first and above all understood as religious freedom. And from this understanding flowed the passion for political and intellectual independence from Europe that bore the nation. The New England Puritans forged a theological culture in the seventeenth century that lasted well over 100 years and set the mold for the country's moral and ethical development. For the Puritans of New England America was the "New Jerusalem," and the basic collective model of their doing was the people and nation of Israel, "the children of Israel," as they are popularly apostrophized in American folklore.

America was Israel, and the Americans were the chosen people; America's future was to be the fulfillment of biblical prophecy. America, the vast, almost empty continent (it is estimated that in the sixteenth century there were fewer than a million Indians in what is now the United States), was obviously the land of the future.

And the future was clear; it had been divinely foreseen, planned, and ordained. It was a matter of "manifest destiny." Cotton Mather began his magnum opus, *Magnalia Christi Americana; or, The Ecclesiastical History of New England,* with these words: "I write the Wonders of the Christian Religion, flying from the depravations of Europe, to the American Strand: and, assisted by the Holy Author of that Religion, I do, with all conscience of Truth, required therein by Him, who is the Truth itself, report the wonderful displays of His infinite Power, Wisdom, Goodness, and Faithfulness, wherewith His Divine Providence hath irradiated an Indian Wilderness."

Thus America was at least as steeped in religion as

Russia was, and it had the inenarrable attraction of the new continent to fire the imagination in addition. "America" is one of the two greatest romantic jags in the history of the world. The other is the Christian religion, Greek East or Latin West. The combination of the two, each with a great continent to work with, is, and has been proved, overpowering. Too, the majesty of the American natural scene combined with the religious habit of mind of its new beholders, who saw the hand of God in every aspect of nature and discerned "remarkable providences" in every manifestation of life in "God's country."

The tendency to see spiritual significance in every natural fact dovetailed neatly with the mysticism of the nature-worshiping American Indians, whose names and place-names very often prevailed over those imposed by their conquerors. Both Puritan spirituality and Indian mysticism pay tribute to the power of "the spirit of the place."

It was all here and settled at the very beginning: American idealism, American morality, American optimism. *"Plus ça change, plus c'est la même chose"*—"the more it changes, the more it remains the same thing," whether in conformity or rebellion. Hawthorne, Melville, and the New England company were the spiritual and intellectual heirs of the Puritans. "America," said G. K. Chesterton, "is a nation with the soul of a church."

Herman Melville, in many ways the American counterpart of Dostoyevsky, was himself a child of the church. He was born and reared in a religious family, went to what is described as "an especially pious school," and listened to a great many sermons, most of them in the Calvinist Dutch Reformed Church. The corpus of his work is suffused with religion. His masterpiece, *Moby Dick*, begins in terms of its first most memorable scene with the sermon of the sailor-preacher Father Mapple. The Bible, principally the Old Testament, actually gives his creative work its structure. Melville struggled all his life with the dogmas of the Calvinist faith. *Moby Dick* is described by the German scholar of American literature Ursula Brumm as "an embittered debate over predestination and free will conveyed in the rebellion of the 'satanic' hero, Ahab." Well, then, what was it Moby Dick conveyed or symbolized? Great, starkly simple, primordial, and terrible as it was and considering how the embittered debate over predestination and free will ended—was this the same force that destroyed Stavrogin, the man of the cross (*stavros* is Greek for "cross")? The same force that laid John Lennon low at the hands of a "Jesus freak"? The same force that girded and steeled Vladimir Ulyanov, using the name Lenin, to murder thousands by direct order and millions by decree?

There is also the interesting parallel between the fates of the two nations in the article of rapid, not to say abrupt, secularization. The abrupt secularization of society is the leitmotiv of Dostoyevsky's work, and it is the literary fate of Melville. In both cases, that of the Soviet Union and that of the United States, the process of secularization which had taken centuries in Europe was compressed into a period well within the life-spans of the two writers. Ursula Brumm cites Melville's attention to the naval encounter between the *Bon Homme Richard* and the English man-of-war *Serapis*. He ascribed to it a "singularly indicatory" significance, saying that "it may involve at once a type, a parallel and a prophecy." He added: "Sharing the same blood with England, and yet her proved foe in two wars—not wholly inclined at bottom to forget an old grudge—intrepid, unprincipled, reckless, predatory, with boundless ambition, civilized in externals but a savage at heart, America is, or may yet be the Paul Jones of nations."

Brumm notes that a great deal of American literary criticism has dealt with the simplicity of American depiction of character and situation compared with the highly individualistic differentiation in plot and characterization typical of the European novel. Significantly, in addition to the simplicity of social texture and the lack of cultural institutions, the democratic equality of America's citizens is cited. The Bible had not only given Melville's work its structure, but also performed the same function for American society and American polity. Without it there ensued a situation which prompted Henry James, Sr., to write in 1859: "Democracy is not so much a new form of political life as a dissolution and disorganization of old forms. It is simply a resolution of government into the hands of the people, a taking down of that which has before existed, and a recommitment of it to its original sources...."

It would appear that the role of religion since the abrupt secularization of American life has been vastly underestimated. Without the role of religion clearly evident, a question immediately arises, against the background of the universal consensus that America is above all (and only) an idea: What's the big idea? No one could write a "Letter to the American Leaders" à la Solzhenitsyn's "Letter to the [Soviet] Leaders": How then a "little America"? To make a little anything out of America, one would first have to change its name.

The overarching, all-informing idea of America is freedom. But freedom is by definition indefinite and indefinable. It is by no means an ordering factor. Without the rudder of religion the American ship of state has zigged and zagged all over the seven seas as various makeshift rudders were fitted into place from time to time. In the highly pluralistic society of America, humanism is no viable substitute.

Humanism too easily contradicts itself. Norman Podhoretz points out, for example, that in recent years the parties in contention over the Scopes trial (the theory of evolution versus Genesis) have reversed their positions. Now, instead of religious fundamentalists and the political right opposing evolution, it is the political left that opposes evolution because of the genetic explanations for human behavior.

The zigzagging of a would-be secular America has hardly gone unnoticed, particularly as regards the Soviet threat. Alois Mertens, state secretary for the German Federal Republic, has remarked that the American perception of it continually vacillates between banalization and demonization. This is a reflection of America's shuttlecock perception of itself, moving almost rhythmically to hubris from self-debasement and back again, lurching from delusions of omnipotence to penance for the same and a groveling protestation of impotence.

Within two weeks after Neil Armstrong had put his foot on the moon, a feat which (meticulously televised) held the world in thrall, the American public had turned its collective attention from the moon shot and the entire American space program to the plight of itinerant grape pickers in California. The attention span of the American public seems to grow shorter with each passing year.

In one of his early essays, Friedrich Nietzsche warned the Swiss Confederation against the dangers of introducing a system of mass education at the expense of the elitist selection—*numerus clausus*—which prevailed in Switzerland before the turn of the century. The dismantlement of the intellectually patrician system, he warned, would inevitably lower the standards of the educational process to the point where it would deliver the Swiss public into the hands of...journalists. Such a catastrophe, he implied, would permanently disable the republic.

In America the Republic was presented at the outset with a *fait accompli*. The American public was at the mercy of journalists, beginning with Tom Paine. Even so, the first Republic of the New World practiced what it preached and placed no intellectual requirements on the increasing numbers of immigrants. Nor does it, to any particular extent, to this day. The result of this general state of affairs has been a free-for-all that has favored, and lavishly, the strong, the quick, the ambitious, and the sly—to put the best possible face on it. America has become a nation of hidden elites and garishly exposed celebrities. It is in the interest of both these groups to endorse and advocate the egalitarian tradition because they, especially, profit from it.

Chapter VII

Matthew Arnold had America directly in view when he passed his judgment on democracy:

> The difficulty for democracy is, how to find and keep high ideals. The individuals who compose it are, the bulk of them, persons who need to follow an ideal, not to set one; and one ideal of goodness, high feeling and fine culture, which an aristocracy once supplied them, they lose by the very fact of ceasing to be a lower order and becoming a democracy. Nations are not truly great solely because the individuals composing them are numerous, free and active, but they are great when these numbers, this freedom, and this activity are employed in the service of an ideal higher than that of an ordinary man, taken by himself.

It would be difficult, indeed, to think of a more eloquent begging of the religious question. As it was, the secularization of America went hand in hand with a

71

series of educational reforms stretching over a century and more and continuing to this day. The egalitarian drive to accommodate the disadvantaged—most particularly and understandably the American blacks—lowered primary, secondary, and higher education standards to the point of ruination of many a school system, perhaps most signally and painfully, the New York City school system. Since the New York City school system was largely the creation and pride of the metropolis's Jewish community, its demolition as an effective institution of learning did no little to poison the already strained relations between Jews and blacks in the city and beyond, indeed far beyond; the New York City school system was generally regarded as one of the best in the country.

The impact of the advent and rapid development of television on the American public at large and on the disadvantaged sections of the public in particular can hardly be exaggerated. Its effect on the moral fiber of the nation was very soon discernible.

Within a very few years much of America's youth was glued to the television screen for a national average of six hours a day. For many of the disadvantaged it became the only effective schooling they were ever to know. By the same token, however, the children of poor families or "half families," especially blacks and Hispanics, were robbed of any incentive to undergo formal schooling. The temptation provided in endless entertainment free of charge (except for the cost of attention to the more and more frequent commercials) decimated school attendance in the poorer sections of the great population centers of the nation and increased the percentage of dropouts by several hundredfold. The combination of television and radically lowered educational standards produced the phenomenon of the illiterate high school graduate and, in some cases, even the illiterate college graduate.

There is also, of course, very much the question of television fare. A few years ago on a panel show (David Susskind's *Open End*) the syndicated columnist Joseph Kraft "acknowledged" that America did not have and did not need a foreign policy. It was better so, he said, because without a foreign policy we could be pragmatic about foreign affairs. Two weeks later on the same show the Reverend William Sloane Coffin asserted that "we don't want leaders, we don't need leaders."

When called to account for this statement, he explained that "we do need spokesmen." He was not asked, and he did not say for whom. Presumably for the people then. In any society the spokesman occupies the pivotal position. He is in the middle, which is, of course, what the word *media* basically means. In a dictatorship the spokesman or official writer is "the engineer of the human soul," as Stalin called him, and he works according to specification handed down from above.

The democratic writer or spokesman is allegedly free of all constraint. He not only interprets but also forms public opinion. Still, with the enormous leverage resultant from the electronic revolution, the television spokesman is subject to the constraint of temptation: He can be Promethean—or Luciferian—not only because the power to enlighten is also the power to deceive but rather because the medium of television has a causal effect on events. The camera makes performers of its subjects just as it makes subjects of its spectators. The magic of the magic box works both ways. It is black magic.

We have the pseudoevent. Who can forget Jackie Robinson's graphic account of H. Rap Brown in a basement in Harlem haranguing five bums—and a CBS television team? To fill the ever-increasing maw of the television industry we also have the pseudoentertainer and the acting character (media personality) instead of the character actor. The shortfall of talent and material in the face of the demand for entertainment produced a species of errant garrulity, a professional aimlessness to fill time. Most dangerous of all, we have the usurpation of the public domain by the entertainer posing as a qualified commentator on national and international events.

For some time now we also have had the opposite phenomenon: the more or less qualified commentator posing as an entertainer on the fun news shows (where everybody laughs most of the time). In either case, with the fatal electronic boost the right of free speech has become the license to kill or create causes to assassinate or apotheosize character (the media's treatment of Henry Kissinger is a two-way example). The source of the evil lies in the discrepancy between the media personality's prestige and his ignorance of the subject matter he deals with. The result is the piracy of prime television time for an uninstructed purpose.

We have spokesmen sure enough. Their name is legion: spokesmen at random by unperceived lateral transfer, regular contributors to what one psychologist has termed "the unfathomable pool of public misinformation." The spoken word has fallen prey to the electronic image. Whereas apprentice newpaper people are told to write to the intelligence level of a fourteen-year-old, the television writer must choose words that will be understood by an eight-year-old.

Before the advent of television there were at least a dozen nationally famous preachers in America: George Buttrick, Harry Emerson Fosdick, Reinhold Niebuhr, Henry Sloane Coffin. Today we have only Billy Graham (Oral Roberts is confined to the regional networks of the South). America used to have speakers, men who were rightly famous for their skill with the spoken word. Apparently the breed died out with Adlai Stevenson and "the Wizard of Ooze," Everett Dirksen.

Can intelligence be divorced from language? "In the beginning was the word." And in the end? What has happened to the American's sense and feeling for the language? "When we get through with the American language," says Artemus Ward's Mr. Dooley, "it will look like it had been run over by a musical comedy!" What does it look like now? What remains of the great American rhetorical tradition? Certainly it no longer resides in American politicians. Gerald Ford took the precaution of informing Congress that he was not much of a speaker: "I'm a Ford," he said, "not a Lincoln."

Indeed, there used to be television critics of note, like John Crosby. Now, as Crosby himself puts it, "There isn't anything left to criticize; it's just *Mission Impossible* over and over again."

"Democracy," said Oscar Wilde, "is the bludgeoning of the people, by the people, for the people." Television is the bludgeon. America continues to be brutalized— now more than ever. And not by means of a conspiracy. There is no considerable conspiracy in the United States. But there is something far more dangerous because it is intangible. It is as if the American people had drifted, normally, naturally, and honestly through a Nietzschean "neurosis of perfect health" into a condition that complements conspiracy.

How many hundreds of thousands, perhaps even a million and more, of young blacks are there, victims of how many thousands of hours before the television screen, with not so much as an idea in their heads, let alone a set of values, to console them for the time wasted, to equip them for any sort of meaningful existence? Why study and prepare for the future when a welfare check will buy a color television set? No education, no skills, no values, no graces, no manners are required for a lifetime of watching the box. Goethe foresaw the effect of television even before the advent of photography:

> Stuff and nonsense can be spoken,
>   Can be written, too,
> Neither bones nor spirit broken
>   By such means untrue.
> Yet the same stuff put in pictures
>   Has its magic thrall,
> Grips the senses in its strictures,
>   Binds the soul withal.

The media personality is the Pied Piper of our time, the true and false representative of the American people. His is at once the creator, the master, and the abject slave of the common man. He exhibits the same lack of direction, the same rejection of discipline; he gives voice to the same idle notions, inconsistent with the least inquiry. He is the mass man of the mass media, individual only in his selfishness. And selfishness is his only real message. He still manages—this is his greatest achievement—to put a pleasant face on greed. In America, not in the Soviet Union, we have something like, but not quite like, the dictatorship of the proletariat. Mass rule of a sort, what we have is a "mediocracy."

Chapter VIII

I asked one of America's foremost television commentators, Howard K. Smith, how he felt about the way America was going. Was he at all alarmed?

"Yes," he said, "I'm alarmed. I think it's doing all right now...people are not hurting. But it is not prepared for the long-term future problems. Armaments alone—the way the Russians have caught up and passed us in arms in ten years has frightened me because the Russians are not kind when they have arms.

"The fact is that innovation used to be a leading American quality. Ten years ago—sixty percent of the major innovations were made by Americans, year for year. That's gone. Western Europe makes more than we do now. The story of the transistor is typical. The transistor, the tiny little thing that allows computers and space travel, was invented in the Bell Laboratories in New Jersey thirty-four years ago. The Japanese took it over, put it into radios, made them better than we did or cheaper than we did—they have run us out of business....

"I have to guess that—this is a terrible thing to say, and it can be misinterpreted; the Russians would love it—but the only nation which truly benefited from World War Two was the United States. We were pulled out of the Depression by it. We built up the most huge production apparatus in history. So when the war was over, we had prosperity everywhere. All our industries were the best. Everyone else's were destroyed. And so I think our managers were mainly to blame for this lack of innovation. They simply gave up. They said, 'we're just so good we needn't worry'... and they got out of the habit of innovation.

"Meanwhile, Germany started from scratch... and produced the most modern industry. Japan went from scratch to the most modern industry. Peripheral nations around Asia are turning into industrial giants: Taiwan, South Korea, Singapore.... And we are just not up to that. We've got to get out of this somehow, we've got to compete... we've got to fight."

Hegel coined the phrase "the impotence of victory"; did Smith mean that winning the war had ruined America?

"It certainly spoiled us. The dollar was all that counted in the world. The American was treated—even allowing for anti-Americanism—all over the world like royalty.... All this was bought with American dollars after World War Two. And I think we were spoiled by that. Now... I blame the managers for that, more than government, more than the workers, more than anyone else...."

But America was still ahead in electronics, I said. Just consider the two-way television city (where set owners could signal back to master control at the TV station), as was the case in Columbus, Ohio.

"Oh," Smith said, "I think there are many which are outstanding still, and the vastest is... agriculture. The farmers are our best industrialists. Do you know they have invented a harvester with one man in the hood? And in this little hood he's got a stereophonic radio, and this thing combs down the sugar beet fields and pulls out three tons of sugar beets in one minute with one man running it—a job that used to involve the work of hundreds of harvesters. . . . So in agriculture we're untouched.

"Every American farmer feeds sixty people. Every West European farmer feeds nineteen. Every Russian farmer feeds nine. So we're still at the top of that. And with computers we really are way out ahead . . . and that is to say, we are ahead in all the space sciences.

"But the management of much of our industry has simply gone lazy and self-satisfied. The farmers of this country last year, in spite of high trade barriers against them, sold twenty-seven billion dollars' worth of American farm goods—that's equal to our whole world trade deficit. They pave the way for all of us. They're outstanding. They produce so much they're in crisis. . . ."

What about the American television industry? I asked.

"We're not ahead there. . . ."

And the future of television in America—all the technical innovations, cable TV, videotapes, videodiscs, would there be as many as thirty or fifty channels?

"I think cassettes are the biggest threat to network television. I think the time may come where there may be in every corner drugstore a section where you can phone in and say, 'Do you have *Star Wars*?' or 'Do you have *Jaws*?'" 'Yes.' 'Well, could you send it around?' "Yes, we can deliver by six—will that be early enough?' 'Yes, and you can pick it up tomorrow morning at nine.' So you will be able to rent it for the night for six dollars. And so instead of watching (network) TV you prepare it yourself. I think that's the threat to the TV networks."

I said my mind boggled at the thought of thirty channels—let alone fifty. So many channels would certainly give a great many actors and technicians work.

"I don't think so," said Smith, "because it costs too much money to produce it. I don't think any channel will earn enough money to pay the bills for it. That's what I thought would happen when TV was invented.

79

I said, 'Now all the scripts will come out of bottom drawers; all the new young dramatists who have been waiting so long will blossom. We're going to see a new age, a new Shakespearean age of drama! Well, we've seen crap...and I think that's what the thirty channels will produce, too—because it costs so much to put out a good production on thirty channels. I think that it will lower the quality of TV to have thirty channels. You know, journalism was never worse in this country than it was at the founding of the Republic. Every city had one hundred and seventy newspapers. All of them were broadsheets—and they were terrible! They treated with sensations, lies! Well, I think that with thirty channels that is what you're likely to get. I think the good threat would be a public broadcasting system which has lots of money, but the commercial threat would be the cassettes....'

What did he think of the quality of the American commercial TV, such as the sitcoms, *Rockford File, Streets of San Francisco*?

"Mostly pretty thin," Smith said, "...there isn't enough imagination to fill even four stations going on the air eighteen hours a day; there just isn't enough imagination around. Shakespeare wrote about forty hours of useful entertainment in his whole lifetime of a genius; the rest of it is trash...."

A good point, I thought, one to be kept in mind in the face of expectations.

"Yes," he said, "you just cannot fill that much time with good stuff. I just regret that we don't try now and then....We did try now and then with *Roots* but...not enough. But the three parts of *Henry VI* just shouldn't be in print they are so bad. *Titus Andronicus*, where they rape a woman and murder seventeen people on the stage—that was pure sensationalism by Shakespeare just to get an audience. It was a lousy play."

I remembered that I had once asked Dick Cavett pretty much the same question: Why it was that in our youth—in the thirties and forties—there were at least a hundred great stand-up comedians in the country. Now there was none.

"The answer is easy," said Cavett, "TV killed them. I remember a famous old vaudeville star who came out of the past and appeared on the *Ed Sullivan Show*. He was a sensation! He bowled everybody over; they had never seen anything like it before. So they asked him to come back for the next week's show. But he couldn't. He didn't have anything left—nothing else. He'd shot his bolt. The point is that in vaudeville a comedian had one turn, and that one turn lasted him for many years, decades, maybe even a lifetime. After all, vaudeville stars traveled all over the country, playing every whistle stop with the same skit every time. Now you play it once on a national hookup, and it's over and done with forever; you're through. That's the difference; that's how TV killed the stand-up comedians."

I then asked Smith the big question for a TV correspondent and commentator: What about the "television war"—the distortion caused by or inherent in American TV coverage of the Vietnam War?

"It was the doing of the Americans," said Smith. "The American army provided everything: They provided transportation to the battlefield; they let you put your cameras over their shoulders to take pictures of what they were doing. Whereas the South Vietnamese were hard to cover—you didn't understand their language; they didn't understand reporters or see why anybody should be there. And the North Vietnamese naturally were the enemy, and you couldn't get close to them. So I think it was the simple ease with which Americans could be shown dying and bloody and beaten, the ease with which Americans could be shown shooting up the local guerrillas who were always dressed as civilians. It was this that created doves. So the ease with which America made itself a victim of that kind of reporting was the cause of the distortion."

It was, then, I said, largely a simple question of access.

"Yes... and I think most Americans want to be liberal, and most of the liberal organizations in America were demonstrating in the streets and in the academic institutions against the war, so they took that stand, too. And also the war was getting a little disgusting...because we were losing.... We had for twenty years paid all our taxes to create the strongest armed force in the world, and here we were faced with an army of a little people of eighteen million, and we refused to use those weapons. So all those things account for the fact that the Americans were a little disgusted with the way the war was being fought: They felt that you shouldn't sacrifice American boys if you weren't willing to support them with all those weapons we paid so much to produce. Then there was the accessibility—seeing Americans suffering unnecessarily and hurting others."

Howard K. Smith had worked for many years with CBS before going to ABC. The switch was caused by a falling-out Smith had had with William Paley, the owner and president of CBS. I asked Smith about this rupture and when it happened.

"In 1961 Paley asked me to write a paper on what our policy is and what it should be, and I drew up a paper analyzing the policy and pointing out that when you report the news, you have to report facts, which are going to lead to conclusions, and the thing is you couldn't avoid it. And he sat me down to lunch and threw my own paper across the table at me and said, 'I've read this kind of stuff before,' and then I said, 'You should look somewhere else.' I don't think he expected me to. I think he expected me to say, 'Well, let's try again,' but I didn't. I shoved myself away from the table and said, 'This conversation is over,' and walked off. I never saw him again."

I interviewed Elie Abel, professor of communications at Stanford University and a member of Sean MacBride's UNESCO commission for the study of the international media, in the same course of inquiry. Struck as I was by Howard K. Smith's statement on the war, I made it my first question to Abel. Did he consider American TV reportage of the Vietnam War slanted?

"I was perhaps a victim of the TV war in a way," said Abel. "At the time I was living in London. I was the senior European correspondent for NBC, which

meant that I basically traveled the circuit from London
to Moscow and the Middle East. Those stories that I
was doing had to compete for air time with combat
footage from Vietnam. And no matter how well turned
a piece, say, about De Gaulle's attitude toward British
entry into the Common Market and other topics that
seemed to us rather important, [it] frequently wound
up on the shelf, essentially because action was the miss-
ing component, I mean, visible action. There's a built-
in problem with TV, it seems to me, as practiced in the
United States. The most interesting stories frequently
are the nonvisual ones. I happened to be a diplomatic,
correspondent. Diplomatic correspondents are most often
reporting what happened in a closed room. If there is
any footage at all, it is posed beforehand, and it doesn't
tell you anything. The content of what happened you
have to discover in nonvisual ways. Now, it's very hard
to tell that kind of story except in the form of what TV
producers call a talking head. And I was the quintessential talking head. No, when you think about it, what
you're trying to report is what is going on inside people's
minds and inside closed rooms. There is nothing visual
about it. I have never discovered a better way to tell
that kind of story than to have a reasonably intelligent,
articulate journalist stand up and say, 'This, I understand, is what happened today,' or, 'This is what we
think it means.'

"That kind of story gets lost too often in the competition for action film. So that kind of story is, I think,
one of the lesser casualties of the Vietnam experience.
And Vietnam also happened to coincide with a certain
amount of riotous activity in the big-city ghettos in the
northern cities of the United States. And there, too, you
had crowds searching in front of the cameras. That kind
of stuff was the raw meat that many TV people were
looking for. And so the more thoughtful, the more in-
trospective kind of report got lost.

"Now on the actual coverage of the war: There was
a terrible sameness to it. It was very hard to cover a
sortie by a group of GIs or marines who were airlifted
by helicopter from one place to another. The chopper

comes down, the tall grass is whipped by the breeze from the rotary blades, and then they march one by one.... It's graphic, and yet it's so repetitive that it doesn't really tell you a great deal about what the Vietnam War was all about. I think there I would fault the reporters not so much for the concentration on action, because that was something their home office demanded, but it seems to me that the political dimension of the war got lost.... A great many people have felt that there was a certain bias in the reporting. Part of that, of course, was built in. Simply the fact that our journalists had access only to our side, and therefore, there was our side dealing out death and destruction. I think it might have been useful if every now and then a reminder was given to the public that this was not a complete picture, that this was a series of snapshots in an area in which snapshots were permitted.

"But I do feel that there is not much question that bombardment day after day of Vietnam in action photographs—some of them horrible because war is horrible—that had a lot to do, I think, with igniting the student protest movement and the events that followed. The curious thing is that some of the young people, including my own students, were blaming the media for not telling the truth.... And yet in a strange way it was the media that made them aware of Vietnam and the nature of the war to a limited extent and turned them into antiwar activists...."

I thought that was an interesting point and said so.

"Well," said Abel, "TV did it in another strange way that I don't think anyone fully understands, and it baffles me. Certainly in that period the flow of news film was from West to East, from America to Europe predominantly. And then on even farther East.... This had some very strange effects. It was to a degree a confirmation, if you will, of McLuhan's 'The medium is the message.'

"Let's put the war aside for just a moment. The counterculture, the notion that a with-it kid had to go unwashed and wear baggy jeans and sandals and all the rest and the life-style that went with it.... It started really with the Berkeley troubles in '65. Those images—mostly with a track laid over them in which a correspondent appreciably older than the kids was making rather disapproving noises about the untidiness of their life-styles—moved in the way that news film does, from California to Chicago to New York to London to Paris and onward.

"The astonishing thing to me was that the life-style caught on almost immediately in the East, and TV pictures must have been certainly the most important contributing element there. I mean it led to scenes I remember when I went to the Free University of Berlin in the winter of 1966 and '67. There was quite a lot of antiwar agitation then, which seemed to me a little odd because Germany wasn't in the war and all of that, but there was quite a lot of it even so.

"I remember standing on a street corner on the Kurfürstendamm when a group of these kids came marching up, wearing blue jeans and sandals without socks—in Berlin in December, which can be pretty blowy, as you know—holding up placards in English, reading, "Make Love, not War,' and one other placard which was even more disturbing to me, which read, 'Vietnam Equals America's Auschwitz.' Leaving aside the political message which may have inspired that, it struck me that they were acting out a scene that they had seen on TV, that they had observed and then imitated in that way. It was the child thing to do; it was the 'in' thing....So I think TV film or videotape today has a great deal to do with influencing ideals of this kind."

Chapter IX

In his speech at the Harvard commencement exercises in 1978, Aleksandr Solzhenitsyn characterized the Western press as follows: "The necessity to provide instantaneous authoritative information constrains [the journalist] to fill the void with guesses, to collect rumors and suppositions, which are then never rectified but remain sticking in the memory of the masses. How many overhurried, precipitous, ill-considered, misleading judgments are pronounced daily, deluding the brain of the reader (or listener) and so to congeal! The press has the possibility of simulating public opinion and the possiblity of feeding it with distortions." This reads like an echo of A. J. Liebling in a piece written for the *New Yorker* in 1960: "The change in title [School of Communications] from the old-fashioned school of journalism underlines the decreasing role of newspapers in the future as envisaged by a busy paper-jobber. The institution will not be called a School of Information, either, I noted without astonishment, or a School of News.

Communication means simply getting any idea across and has no intrinsic relation to truth. It is neutral. It can be a peddler's tool, or the weapon of a political knave or the medium of a new religion."

The increasing predominance of television as *the* communications medium has not only radically reduced the number of commentaries and editorials effectively available to the public, but virtually removed a whole dimension of the news—namely, the political dimension. The American press is open to manipulation from all sides. Its very nature leads to the privatization of the public means of communication.

"What appears to be practiced by many," wrote John Calvin in his letter "On God and Political Duty" to Francis I of France, "soon obtains the force of custom.... And human affairs have scarcely ever been in so good a state as for the majority to be pleased with things of real excellence. From the private vices of multitudes, therefore, has arisen public error, or rather a common agreement of vices, which these good men would now have to receive as law."

Television has catapulted the practice of the many into a prominence Calvin could not possibly have foreseen. With the proportionate decrease in commentary and analysis of the news, this branch of journalism has devolved on columnists. Perhaps the frequent appearance of prominent columnists on television, where they are obliged to provide ad hoc opinions and hip-shot commentaries, accounts for the falling off in the quality of the product.

The capitalist system turns on the sell—on the seduction of the consumer. The consumer is free to refuse the pitch, if he can. This means that all the more effort is spent to seduce him since the free enterprise system of competitive selling demands it. So the appeal—and many of the best minds in America are wholly engaged in making it as effective as possible—is reduced to the principles of utility and pleasure, which are the lowest common denominators in civilized society. In this way American society and with it more or less the whole of

Western society have backed into an all-embracing triviality.

It would be hard to exaggerate the importance of the press and television to modern terrorism. Terrorists exploit the inevitably forthcoming publicity to use murder as an instrument of political power with increasing effect. The coverage afforded the hostage takers occupying the American embassy in Teheran, particularly by American television crews, did more to increase the political leverage of the hostage takers and weaken the position of the American government, than any other factor involved.

The television networks' practice of announcing after each evening's prime time news broadcast the ever-increasing how-manyeth day of the hostage holding unnecessarily exacerbated public feeling and brought added pressure on the American government. In American democracy the public domain is strictly the province of private enterprise; the ownership of the means of production, including the production of ideas and opinion and their dissemination, is in private hands. In American journalism, which has developed without the sheet anchor of a long-established tradition (not to mention the Official Secrets Act) enjoyed by the British, this has made for a kind of chaos.

A. J. Liebling recounts in part how this chaos came about: "... the newspapers decided not to represent particular persuasions. Instead, they proposed to report evenhandedly on all of them and their controversies. Thus they introduced the tutelage of impartiality, which endowed the editors with the power to determine which position should be brought before the public eye, and how vigorously." This was a foundation stone of the present policy. It is clear enough in general that the newspapers' decision to publish news at the expense of anything else was dictated by the expense of publishing anything else but the news.

Still, if the American media are in large part guided by the laws of the market, there is one cause that American journalism vigorously sustains. This, as Walter

Cronkite has put it, is the journalists' discharge of "their role as independent and fearless monitors of the public's servants." This is the primary function of the press in America: to see to it that the state is held accountable. The press performs this function by exposing the government and its workings to the public eye. The press insists on immunity in the article of its sources, on the right not to reveal its sources, thus maintaining its corner of secrecy, which constitutes the essence of its independence from the state. In a 1973 interview in *Playboy* Cronkite said that most newsmen tend to be "liberal and possibly left of center as well.... They come to feel little allegiance to the established order. I think that they're inclined to side with humanity rather than with authority and institutions." Then he added, "We're big. And we're powerful enough to thumb our nose at threats and intimidation from government. I hope it stays that way." This might be called adversary journalism or indeed random adversary journalism.

Here is Walter Cronkite again: "I don't think it is any of our business what the moral, political, social or economic effect of our reporting is.... We should not decide what is good and what is bad for people. ...Because then people are denied the information that democracy entitles them to have." (It is interesting to compare Cronkite's formula with the credo of another age. "What is right," wrote William Randolph Hearst, "can be achieved through the irresistible power of awakened and informed public opinion. Our object, therefore, is not to enquire whether a thing can be done, but whether it ought to be done, and if it ought to be done to so exert the forces of publicity that public opinion will compel it to be done.")

The American media's obsession with the news equates with the Soviet state's obsession with "espionage" (which is merely the news in general and the news the Soviets do not consider fit to print or broadcast in particular). The American media, incidentally, regard the American intelligence community as their only rival in the collection and brokerage of information.

But do the media deliver "the information that democracy entitles them [its readers, listeners, and viewers] to have"?

Walter Cronkite has declared that he was "not bound by doctrines or committed to a point of view in advance." Yet he was quoted in the *Utica Press* (November 13, 1974) as saying, "There are always groups in Washington expressing views of alarm over the state of our defenses. We don't carry these stories. The story is that there are those who want to cut defense spending." This is a paraphrase of David Brinkley's straightforward statement: "News is what I say it is. It's something worth saying by my standards." And here is an excerpt from a column dated October 1979 by Albert Shanker, the president of the United Federation of Teachers:

> Much of what is taught and learned in social studies does not come from textbooks. It comes from newspapers, radio and television.... A few weeks ago there was a rumor that the Beatles might come together again for a concert to benefit the Vietnamese "boat people." The story made big headlines and television reports and no doubt was discussed by millions of students... even though it anticipated an event which did not happen. The Beatles did not reunite. At about the same time, there was another reunion, not rumor but fact. More than sixty survivors of Soviet labor camps, prisons and psychiatric jails came together. There were the great and the famous—Sinyavsky, Amalrik, Bukovsky, Ginsburg, Grigorenko, Chalidze, Litvinov, Maximov and Mrs. Alexander Solzhenitsyn. And there were others, too, ordinary citizens and workers who had been trapped in the Soviet system. They came from their new homes, cities all across America, Europe, Israel. But this event our nation's press, with a few notable exceptions, chose not to cover in any serious, sustained fashion.... In a special message that Andrei Sakharov sent to the hearings, he emphasized that in the fight for human rights throughout the world, the same criteria must be applied "with full political and ideological objectivity" to all countries, and that non-

violent methods—"namely openness and publicity"—should be "the main weapon." The problem is
that far too often (as the P.L.O., the I.R.A. and other
terrorist groups know), "publicity" doesn't flow from
non-violence and "openness"—unless, like the Bea-
tles rumor story, it's a question of "show biz." Most
Americans were not told by the papers they read or
the television programs they watch that the Sakharov hearings were even being held—and even more
rarely did the moving, frightening testimony of those
hearings get to the printed page.

At the beginning of the Sakharov hearings in Washington, the committee in charge was informed that the
Washington Post editors had decided in conference that
the hearings were not news. (While the hearings were
in progress, a rather modest story on them appeared in
the society section of the *Post*.) The decision that the
hearings were not news was reached not because the
majority of the editors of the *Post* are leftist but because
the categorical alignment of the East European dissidents with the American government lumps the dissidents with the American establishment and hence
renders them and most of their doings unacceptable to
the American media. As contradistinct from the Soviet
media, the American media are out to criticize the government, not to praise and popularize it.

Chapter X

The Communist and capitalist systems are as opposite and complementary as the two sides of a coin. It is not just that communism is basically a political approach to economics while capitalism is an economic approach to politics. (Richard von Weizsäcker, former lord mayor of West Berlin and current president of the Federal Republic of West Germany, has contended that capitalism is only an economic theory and wants a political system to supplement it. He did not add that the nature of capitalism predetermines the kind of political system that would supplement, not destroy, it.) The Soviet writer, the Soviet journalist in particular, is an advertising man, a political huckster whose product is a blurb designed to popularize the regime. The American advertising man's blurb is a product of an industry that feeds off and feeds into industry at large. The Communist is out to sell the system; the capitalist is out to systematize the sell. But the counterpoint between the two systems and their respective styles ramifies endlessly. Even the opponents of the two systems stand opposed to each other.

There is a gulf between the two sides, between the social justice espoused by the Communists and the traditional civil rights of the Western democracies. The alignments on either side of the gulf constitute a confrontation within a confrontation between East and West. The left-liberal opposition to the American establishment is aligned ideologically with the Soviet establishment. Angela Davis goes to Prague and denounces Alexander Dubček and his colleagues of the Prague Spring as common criminals. Soviet dissidents arrive in the West by the thousands and side generally with the more or less conservative elements in their host countries. How could Vladimir Bukovsky, after spending twelve of his thirty-five years in Soviet prisons and psycho clinics, have dinner with Margaret Thatcher? Because upon closer acquaintance the left liberals of Britain would have none of him, nor he aught of them. Miss Davis honors Prague because in her view the Czech government champions social rights; Bukovsky dines with Prime Minister Thatcher because she stands for civil rights. These are the two kinds of freedom: from material want and from constraint. There is an essential common element. Because both involve individuals, it is the bedrock of the definition of the two words *freedom* and *individual*. The element is privacy.

In a totalitarian state the striving of the state for total control makes privacy look like clandestinity. By definition privacy cannot be known and therefore cannot be controlled. For this reason in a totalitarian society it is potential treason. Since friendship tends to be a private matter, friendships are latent conspiracies. This is why Communist and fascist regimes try to organize the whole of life into official and semiofficial group activities, into collectives, into public organizations, such as the mass friendship societies, that are amenable to control by the state apparatus.

In a totalitarian state it is extremely difficult to practice espionage. But because the private sector is regarded in principle as clandestine, espionage is potentially and—to the Communist mind—therefore literally omnipresent. The desire and striving for privacy in a totalitarian state of necessity become so active that they equate with clandestinity. Hence the eternal call for vigilance.

The totalitarian state itself generates clandestinity by its perpetual struggle against privacy. The collective, which involves every place of employment, is the totalitarian state's supreme instrument of control. One does not have to be a government spy or stool pigeon by mission, commission, or co-option. Members of a collective are government spies by virtue of their membership in the collective. Soviet administrative law on the power of the USSR KGB authorizes the Ministry of Internal Affairs (MVD) and the KGB to require the cooperation of any person working in a state enterprise.

Since all enterprises are owned by the state, the law is comprehensively applicable. Paragraph 2, entitled "The Classification of Soviet Government Employees," states that "the operational workers of the organs of the USSR Committee for State Security [KGB] are representatives of power."

These do not only perform material technical operations and legal functions but are also granted the right to give obligatory instructions for execution to those who are not subordinated to them. The representatives of power are: deputies [of the Supreme and Local Soviets], government officials, procurators, judges, operational workers of the organs of the USSR Committee for State Security and USSR Ministry of Internal Affairs, representatives of government inspections, and others. The policeman on duty and the district inspector of police are representatives of power. Therefore the authority of the representatives of power have [sic] not only persons who occupy executive or responsible positions but even ordinary employees who perform power functions while executing government assignments, for example, in the preservation of public order.... The representatives of power employ measures of admin-

istrative force on persons who are not subordinated
to them in their line of work.

Soviet citizens who enjoy the rare privilege of traveling abroad, and the even rarer privilege of traveling
abroad repeatedly, carry out tasks for the KGB. Such
service is part of the price of the ticket. The chances
are that the service involved will be a small one, such
as contacting some member of the Russian emigration
and delivering a message, usually a warning, and the
chances are even that if the service to be performed is
at all delicate, the courier will be a prominent concert
artist, writer, painter, or other professional.

This sort of thing is understood and accepted even
by the dissidents, but there is an indistinct line beyond
which such service is considered grounds for openly
branding the traveler concerned as a KGB agent. The
line is indistinct because the dissidents themselves are
usually not in agreement on who is and is not to be
considered an agent. But the government practice of
enlisting the entire working population as active
or passive spies determines the official attitude; and
also the official attitude to the reverse phenomenon—
namely, travelers to the Soviet Union. In the Soviet
Union all tourists are spies.

In the Western democracies, on the contrary, the
abundance of freedom tends to make clandestinity look
like privacy. It is comparatively easy to conduct espionage because clandestinity receives the same sanction
as privacy. Because Americans are so much involved
in privacy, few have any clear notion of the extent to
which it is protected in their country. A recent Supreme
Court ruling, for example, found it illegal for a policeman to stop and check a private automobile unless the
driver is visibly responsible for, or justifiably suspected
of, some irregularity. Justice Byron White ruled: "A
person does not lose all reasonable expectation of privacy simply because the automobile and its use are
subject to government regulation."

In the American-Soviet cultural exchange program

American authorities have not, in most cases, protested actions of the Soviet exchange students and scholars since, while they certainly come under the heading of espionage in the Soviet Union, they are not regarded as espionage in America. In America all spies are tourists.

Whether to regard tourists as spies or spies as tourists depends on one's attitude toward the stuff that makes up information. In general, the media of the Soviet Union report only good news—that is, news that is favorable to the Soviet regime and its policies. Indeed, it is more than good news; it is ideological exhortation to work harder and better, to open up the superb vistas awaiting the workers and peasants under communism. The Soviet media shun bad news as they do the plague, as a matter of principle not reporting airplane crashes (an interesting background to their failure to report their shooting down of KAL Flight 007 punctually or appropriately), train wrecks, or even earthquakes. They were twenty-four hours late in reporting the death of their head of state, Yuri Andropov, after trying for months to pass off his final illness as a cold. (For the Soviets the death of a leader is per se a highly unpleasant and awkward business. Here the Soviet penchant for pomp and circumstance militates against the interests of the Soviet state; a reminder of the vanity of human wishes is also a reminder of the transience of the Soviet system.)

Once again, they adhere as strictly as they can, and more strictly than they should, to Lenin's concept of socialist realism, reporting "Not what is, but what should be." In other words, the editorial policy of the Soviet media is the exact opposite of that of the Western and, particularly, American media. In the West no news is good news and good news is no news. Good weather is not news in the West (it *is* in the Soviet Union!), but a tornado or a hurricane that levels an entire region—*that* is news.

There is a very broad background to this state of affairs. It is undeniably true that there exists in the

West, in the great industrial nations particularly, an unquenchable lust for the sensational, the lurid, the salacious, the catastrophic. The Viennese reader (among multimillions of others in the West, but he particularly) does not feel he has had his due, his "heart starter" to set him up for the day, if his morning newspaper does not headline some frightful catastrophe. This is known as the "end-of-the-world-every-morning editorial policy" guaranteed to titillate the somewhat jaded sensitivities of the overfed burgher of the middle Danubian basin. The surprising thing is that it works every time. There would be severe withdrawal symptoms on a mass scale if the practice were ever to be discontinued.

At the end of each year the media, traditionally, have a round up of the year's major stories and try to divine what their larger significance may be. It is the only time that the media are likely to indulge in any meaningful reflection. On such an occasion three years ago the *Financial Times* revealed that the British press, itself included, had been diametrically wrong over the previous ten years in its reporting on the national standard of living. In the teeth of the unrelievedly pessimistic reporting, the British standard of living had risen steadily and even spectacularly in all categories: TV set, refrigerator, washing machine, freezer, telephone, et al.

At the end of the last year an editorialist of the *Frankfurter Allgemeine Zeitung* wondered what had happened to the gigantic oil slick in the Persian Gulf. For months on end in midyear the media was full of the catastrophe caused by bombardment in the Iran-Iraq War: A thousand tons of oil was flowing daily into the gulf, feeding a slick that was already the size of the state of Baden-Württemberg and threatening to cover an area "half the size of the Baltic Sea." Then, in autumn, there appeared a story under the headline HAS THE OIL SLICK IN THE GULF DISAPPEARED? The story implied that the slick had never really been there in the first place. Since then there hasn't been a word about it. The *Allgemeine Zeitung*'s editorialist found the absence of any protest in the press more alarming than the hoax itself and sought an explanation for the hoax and the absence of protest.

H. L. Mencken answered the first question sixty years ago under the rubric "the problem of false news." He asked:

> How does so much of it get into the American newspapers, even the good ones? Is it because journalists, as a class, are habitual liars, and prefer what is not true to what is true? I don't think it is. Rather, it is because journalists are, in the main, extremely stupid, sentimental, credulous fellows.... The New York Times did not print all its famous blather and balderdash about Russia because the honorable Mr. Ochs desired to deceive his customers, or because his slaves were in the pay of Russian reactionaries, but simply and solely because his slaves, facing the elemental professional problem of distinguishing between true news and false, turned out to be incompetent.

As for the second problem:

> to undertake an overhauling of the faulty technic, and of the incompetent personnel responsible for it.... What lies in the way of it is simply the profound, maudlin sentimentality of the average American journalist—his ingenuous and almost automatic belief in everything that comes to him in writing. One would think that his daily experience with the written word would make him suspicious of it; he himself, in fact, believes fondly that he is proof against it. But the truth is that he swallows it far more often than he rejects it, and that his most eager swallowing is done in the face of the plainest evidence of its falsity. Let it come in by telegraph *from a press association* and down it goes at once.

But the determining factor of the nature of the news in our time is something else. Marx was wrong in his theory of surplus value. The value of a piece of merchandise depends only on whether or not it will sell. If it cannot be sold, it is worthless. The warehouses of the Soviet Union are full of goods and articles that will never be sold.

The founding fathers of communism made a fatal mistake when they failed to codify a penalty for sales resistance. It is the one form of resistance no dictatorship can suppress. Americans know that better than most people. But the Americans—and the West with them—are caught in their own net. If the product of the Soviet writer and journalist is advertising in an overwhelmingly political system, then the product of the American journalist is an article of merchandise in an overwhelmingly commercial system. The product, the news, not only is for sale but *must* be sold. Even men of literature are subordinate to this same commercial force majeure—or what is the meaning of "best seller"? The crepe-hanging, running-everything down, perennial "bad news" jag of the Western media is predetermined by this principle of salability: Good news sells bad; bad news sells good.

Why is this? There are, of course, various reasons, such as the already mentioned watchdog role so dear to the American media: The American journalist is here to blame Caesar, not to praise him—a homegrown Caesar, that is; he is sometimes lavish with his praise of foreign Caesars. This public watchman function explains a good deal about why the journalist writes predominantly bad news, but gives no clue to why the public avidly accepts and even demands it. Both the supply of and the demand for bad news are due basically to a state of affairs in the West that bears a striking resemblance to Lenin's socialist realism: "not what is, but what should be." This is the world of commercial advertising which is based on the theory "What you can make people believe is true, *is* true."

Advertising, says Wyndham Lewis, is a pure expression of the romantic mind. There is nothing so "romantic" as advertising. Here it is important to emphasize the theoretic expression of Western advertising which bears the imprimatur of Dr. Emil Coué. Everything is bigger, better, brighter than ever before. Dr. Coué began his career as a psychotherapist, significantly enough, as a result of responding to an advertisement. Coué's "optimism-to-order" ("Every day in every way I grow better and better") is, as Lewis points out, perfectly in line with the political optimism-to-order of the Western democracies. Indeed, the phenomenon of modern advertising is generally regarded as something peculiarly American, as an outgrowth and expression of the essential nature of America—exuberance, skyscrapers, the obsession with breaking records, "Excelsior!" and "How to make bigger and better elephants!" plus the carefreeness of the American as consumer, his living in-the-moment and for-the-moment.

Chapter XI

The American election campaign in general and presidential conventions in particular are certainly among the most intense and blatant advertising campaigns of our time. (And without, *nota bene*, the restraining hand of the Federal Trade Commission since here the First Amendment takes precedence over codes of acceptable advertising practice. This is an ominous trend that may well account in some part for the advertising mentality of American politicians.) The point to be made here is that in Western public consciousness advertising has almost totally impounded the positive side of life. Advertising has monopolized the good news. It has also laid claim to the insouciant, live-for-the-moment, unthinking American ("fat, dumb, and happy"), the polyp of mass consumerism.

Now, there is nothing the true journalist fears so much as advertising! (Propaganda is advertising for a hidden purpose.) The American journalist constantly suspects himself—and his readers suspect him anyway—of the *hype*, of advertising on the sly. If he says something good about anything—the weather in Arizona, for example (where the weather *is* good almost all the time)—he has to ask himself: "Who might use this for promotion purposes? The Arizona State Chamber of Commerce? The mayor of Phoenix? Or John Smith for his own private aggrandizement of some sort?" So the American journalist and all his Western colleagues sheer off; they avoid the hype like the plague, shy away from it as a horse shies away from fire. There is also the desire—on the part of both the journalist and his readership—to distinguish and dissociate oneself from the "booboisie," from the great American clunk, the sucker who would buy everything he sees advertised if he could.

As a result, the democratic West is polarized between the adman and the bad man—that is, between the advertising man and the bad-news man, the journalist. Since all the good news is in advertising—which is phony, all the real news is bad—the fact that it is bad is the only guarantee of its authenticity. This is socialist realism turned inside out. The Soviets live in a world of bad advertising and good news that is untrue; Westerners live in a world of good advertising and bad news that is by no means entirely true.

So the confrontation between the Soviet Union and the democratic West is a very strange one. We have a Western public addicted to bad news as the only hallmark of reality. We have a Western press and media that trade on bad news as a necessity dictated by that "reality." (The truth is, probably, that in the matter of dosage the bad news is almost as false as the good news.) Western journalists have become something like the bad conscience of the free world. As a result, both the media and the Western public are in a sort of semi-complicity with the Soviet Union. So the West is fighting a spiritual war on two fronts: against the Soviet Union and, in part, against itself—for the Soviet Union.

Historically the process of secularization foreclosed the millennia and rewards in heaven promised by

Christianity, Islam, and other major religions, compensating for the loss by developing or allowing the development of nonreligious prophetic systems of government. (Communism even claimed a higher moral position by referring to the religion it replaced as "the opiate of the people." Significantly, some sixty years later Raymond Aron turned the tables by branding communism "the opium of the intellectuals.") The secularizing process took place in both the Russian Empire and in America with, historically, breathtaking speed, within the life-span of each country's most famous writer: in Russia Dostoyevsky, in America Melville.

In Russia Christianity was replaced by communism, a revolutionary romanticism masquerading as dialectical materialism, promising, as a matter of "scientific certainty" and "historical necessity," the establishment of an earthly paradise for peasants and workers. In America, the New World and "the country of unlimited opportunities," a vaulting commercial romanticism proclaimed and then demonstrated the creation of a mass consumers' paradise "with liberty and justice for all." (The claim of justice was not entirely spurious since the country offered a better chance—to the hardy and adventurous—just as today Miami offers a better chance to make money to the Cuban, despite all attendant difficulties, than does Havana.)

Advertising is the inevitable product of free enterprise. Socialist realism (Communist propaganda) is political advertising because on an international scale communism must compete with other political systems. Commercial advertising has profound social, ethical, and aesthetic consequences. It is not just another economic theory, as Richard von Weizsäcker would apparently have us believe. It unerringly entails a mass consumer life-style and tends strongly to preempt any sort of teleological or cultural—in the classical sense—considerations by concentrating exclusively on the here and now ("All your problems solved for $37.50").

These are the two compensatory prophetic systems developed in East and West in the face of the loss of belief in a just God and a reward hereafter. "Man does not live by bread alone"; no, he lives by catchwords, buzz words in the American vernacular. A prophetic system, of course, is not merely a political system; it is also, perhaps even primarily, an ersatz religion. It is for these reasons that Solzhenitsyn takes the field against both systems. Here it is noteworthy that Octavio Paz, the Mexican writer and critic, hailed (or rebuked) Solzhenitsyn, stating that his most memorable achievement was the destruction of utopia: utopia, literally "no place" (too good to be true), the secular substitute for heaven. *Mutatis mutandis*: Specifically, utopia is the belief that society's ills can be healed by a rational philosophy. The destruction of the latest bastion of that belief—for all political dogmatists this was the Soviet Union—was the work of Solzhenitsyn. His very coinage of the word *gulag*, from the acronym of the official Soviet designation—*Glavnoe upravlenie lagerei*—("Main Directory of Camps") was the trumpet of doom for the leftists and dogmatic humanists in the West. But Solzhenitsyn's revelation will only turn such partisans the more against the system of good advertising and bad news. The reduction of all save the American model spurs their hatred of the American model, nothing more and nothing less.

With these contours of the confrontation in evidence it becomes increasingly clear that the American model finds itself—psychologically—in a no-win situation. The entire struggle between revolutionary romanticism and commercial romanticism turns on a paradox reminiscent of the overworked foreign correspondents' joke during the sixties: "Whoever wins Africa loses the cold war!" All the Soviets have to do is stand fast. That may not be easy to do—in the long run it may not even be possible—but it is simple. The Americans, on the other hand, must bear the brunt of the main controversy and as the confrontation continues, the hullabaloo will increase, and most of it will be in the West.

The Soviet Union can accept the granting of trade and aid to its various satellites and rely on force majeure to keep them more or less in line for the foreseeable future. They can rely on the Germans on both sides of the common German border to preserve the peace. Indeed, the Germans—both East and West—have become the main guarantors for peace for the simple reason that any heightening of tension between the two superpowers will tend to promote a further rapprochement between the two Germanys, with reunification the ultimate goal. Only the peace of Europe guarantees the division of Germany.

Nor do the Soviets have any great cause for concern as regards Western European unity. The Common Market has been deadlocked for a full year over the problem of repayment for past contributions from Great Britain, to name but one of its numerous major difficulties. New candidates clamor for entry and are reluctantly admitted into a highly imperfect economic union, thus foiling any hope of a badly needed and long-overdue consolidation. The political unification is even farther off. "The United States of Europe" is a fading vision curiously unattractive and uninteresting to European youth.

Chapter XII

Recently, alarmed by increasingly blatant public disinterest in the idea of a United Europe, the chancellor of West Germany and the president of France, at one of their regular meetings decided to abolish all border controls between the two countries and announced as much. The announcement caused a great deal of confusion, with customs officials jumping acrobatically out of the way of cars speeding through border checkpoints for several days thereafter.

Helmut Kohl's and François Mitterrand's appropriate offices subsequently announced that it would take some time to dismantle the border checks altogether. Indeed, it has taken almost thirty years already, and there are no signs of any progress whatever. The Common Market has still not achieved its much-heralded customs union. Tariff walls have not disappeared and are not likely to. This is because the tax structures of the various member nations are different. Until they are equalized (a quintessentially political decision), compensatory adjustments at the member nations' borders must be made.

The Common Market's main problem—in delicious counterpoint to the Soviet economy's main problem—is a chronic agricultural surplus. The German government has found itself stuck these many years with subsidizing French farmers for an annual average of 1.5 billion marks (compare this with the 48-billion-ruble—not marks—annual Soviet subsidy for meat and dairy products). When the subsidy threatened to become institutionalized some ten years ago, the Germans protested vehemently. They are still protesting.

To go back a bit, it could have been collusion. In order to keep Germany divided, elaborate alliances were constructed on each side of the dividing line—NATO to the west and the Warsaw Pact to the east. To ensure durability these alliances had to be buttressed with economic systems—EEC to the west and COMECON to the east. In this way the American and the Soviet spheres of interest were secured—magnetic fields with the two superpowers as opposite poles, the force or attraction of which was calculated to be strong enough to keep the two halves of Germany apart indefinitely.

But it is as if the little bit of "Europe" that has been achieved has worked as an inoculation against the idea as a whole. The Common Market has become a technical affair (a highly technical affair), primarily a framework for businessmen. (It reminds one of what Kurt Schumacher, the first postwar Social Democratic leader, called Western Europe: "The breeding ground of capitalism, clericalism and cartels.") The result is a stalemate of conflicting feelings and conflicting interests. "What we actually have here," said a seasoned Eurocrat in Brussels, "is a free trade area with an increasing number of border violations."

The idea of a European defense community, defeated in the French Chamber of Deputies under the premiership of Pierre Mendès-France thirty years ago, was recently disinterred by Franz Josef Strauss in a speech before the Bavarian Defense Committee. A week later during a television panel discussion Strauss admitted that he was well aware how far into the future the realization of such a project needs must be. In Europe the Soviets have every reason to proceed as evenly and quietly as possible. Europe is in disarray, in the doldrums of lack of purpose disturbed only by fits of pique at its own collective impotence. It would be a major mistake on the part of the Soviets to do anything radical enough to stir it to corrective action.

But there is a European purpose that is trying to take shape, slowly coming into tentative formulations in public utterances. Its current form is a variation on the old NATO theme of the two evenly matched columns: Europe and the United States linked to each other from either side of the *mare nostrum*, the Atlantic Ocean. This theme was a favorite of the late Fritz Erler, in his time (the late fifties and early sixties) the military expert of the German Social Democrats. It was meant then, as it is now, as a means of establishing a balance between the American and European forces in the alliance. The theory was, and is, that an equal distribution of power, responsibility, and authority between the two would strengthen the alliance. Europe would at last be making a contribution appropriate to its size of population, industrial capacity, and general prestige.

Nothing precisely like a distinct reassertion of this goal has yet been made, but it is coming. A flurry of ancillary or tangential statements at present points in this direction and dovetails neatly with the outspoken desire of the European allies to have a bigger say in NATO. The outspokenness of the Europeans on this subject is itself an expression of their disenchantment with American leadership at least since Watergate and especially since the unfolding of the Carter administration in its full fatuity. It is also an expression of the fact that there is no longer a consensus on defense and foreign policy in most of the European countries in the alliance.

It is generally overlooked that a strengthening of the European column of the alliance would decrease the dependency of Europe on the United States. Eu-

rope's dependency for its security on the United States
is the cement that holds together the alliance. Independence means detachment. Detachment would provide the Europeans with the freedom of action to ally
themselves with whomever they pleased or to adopt a
stance of armed neutrality.

Not that there is any imminent danger of European
NATO members' actually taking the necessary steps to
reach the goal of independence. The goal is almost as
distant as the European defense community. Here again
the no-win situation of the United States is highlighted.
In all likelihood NATO will stumble along in its present
disarray and disaccord. The Europeans will finally assert themselves and so either paralyze or dissolve the
alliance. What remains is the unforgettable statement
of General Lucius Clay in Berlin in 1961: "Whenever
I try to do anything it goes to the NATO Council where
after several weeks of wrangling, something finally
emerges—the voice of Denmark cautioning restraint."
It is difficult to believe that this situation will improve
as a result of Europe's achieving greater independence
from its chief ally.

Indeed, European defense spending will have to double if Western Europe means to set up a credible independent nuclear and conventional deterrent. This is
the finding of a survey commissioned by the European
Movement, an independent organization that promotes
better cooperation and more political unity within the
Common Market. "An independent Western European
defense, without the United States, would be a very
costly and irreparable mistake," the survey states. "It
would diminish security, increase the costs, and probably enhance the political divisions in Europe." The
survey points out that the cost of an independent European nuclear force coupled with a conventional force
equal to the current U.S. presence in Europe would run
to $400 billion in investment and an annual operating
cost of $100 billion. This would not include the cost of
replacing U.S. reserve units which under present plans
would be flown into Europe in case of war with the
Soviet Union. The survey concludes with the claim that

the alliance with the United States is "the most realistic and responsible option for Western Europe." It also says that the European NATO countries should increase their defense role in any case, recommending that Western European diplomats take part in the intermediate range nuclear forces (INF) arms limitation talks in Geneva when and if they resume.

It is extremely unlikely, since it presupposes unanimous Western European agreement on the subject, that the European NATO members could or would bestir themselves to mount an effort of such magnitude. Hence this survey strongly indicates that American forces will remain in Europe at least until the end of this century.

Chapter XIII

The paradox in the confrontation between revolutionary romanticism, manifested in the Soviet Union, and commercial romanticism, manifested in the United States, is that the weakness of the Soviet Union emerges as its strength while the strength of the United States emerges as its weakness. Let us take the continuing (continuing these many years!) tidal wave of "Americanization" that has flooded Europe and the rest of the world, with very few areas excepted.

Beginning with the Jazz Age and F. Scott Fitzgerald in Paris, Hemingway all over Europe and Africa, and the meteoric rise and fixed-star ascendancy of Hollywood (which, thanks to American supremacy in international television fare, is more popular than ever; the Oscar award ceremonies have become a cult event in Europe and probably elsewhere), the lay culture of the American continent has conquerred the world (to the infinite disgust and resentment of the world's intellectuals). The ramifications of this influence—from "rock" to "big beat" to "pop" to "punk rock"—are difficult to fathom and follow in their entirety. As far as Europe, including Eastern Europe and the Soviet Union, is concerned, the situation is one of almost total immersion.

In a roadhouse in Burgundy the selection list of the jukebox reveals that 91 of the 100 songs listed are American. In the late fifties the East German regime tried desperately to resist the wave of Americanization by introducing and attempting to promote a dance step called the *Lipsi* (from Leipzig). King Canute looked good by comparison.

On a different level, the Soviet Union tried to introduce a traditional Russian soft drink to West Berlin in the early seventies. The "kvass campaign" lasted only one summer. Now, kvass, which is made from brown bread, is an excellent drink. But the Soviets have very little understanding of merchandising—how to package, bottle and dispense, promote, research markets, and the like.

On the other side of the confrontation, many an American soldier during World War II noticed how close the Coca-Cola Company was behind the fighting troops. Within a very few months after the end of the war in Europe, Coca-Cola factories had sprung up as if by magic out of the ground in various locations throughout the American occupation zone in West Germany. This was for the supply of the American troops in Germany and Europe and served as the foundation for the network of Coca-Cola factories in West Germany and West Berlin today. In 1978 the Coca-Cola Company celebrated its triumphal entry into the People's Republic of China. "Coca-colonization" had already taken place in Poland and in the Soviet Union.

The Coca-Cola bottle, like Andy Warhol's painting of a can of Campbell's tomato soup, has become an universally recognized symbol of American power and identity not unlike the American flag in its exclusive significance. As a matter of logical consequence the free enterprise system makes its best showing in the economic field; the American flag follows the American businessman, not vice versa. The Coca-Cola bottle has become an advertisement of itself. And advertising is the strong point of the American system. It comes naturally, and it speaks for itself.

Indeed, the romance inherent in American advertising is catching. It is far more infectious than American attempts to pontificate politically, to propagandize "the American way" or to conduct "psychological warfare" for whatever purpose. This is the positive, cutting edge of American influence as difficult to fend off as a "Big Mac attack." It is here that the loosely bridled genius of the Americans asserts itself as a predominantly commercial phenomenon. They would do well to keep it that way in the confrontation with the Soviet Union because Communists everywhere have great difficulty in coming to terms with economics.

Take the American coinage "standard of living," which is a direct derivative of the American dream become reality. In the East German *Dictionary of Marxist-Leninist Sociology*, 1969 edition, "standard of living" is defined as follows: "its level and direction of development are determined definitively by the state of development of the productive forces and the character of the conditions of production. In bourgeois sociology the concept of a standard of living is more narrowly defined. It describes above all the areas of individual consumption." The second edition of the same work in 1977 defines "standard of living" as "individual consumption as the established measure of supply and demand." In short, in eight years the Communist authorities of East Germany had accepted and even amplified the bourgeois definition while scrapping the gobbledy-gook of "scientific socialism."

The shift herein evident represents a major victory in the universal struggle. Here the Communists were forced by the weight of economic circumstances to adopt a key Western concept relating not to what should be but to what is—or is not—in the here and now. This is the American hallmark and the entrance into the American dream-become-reality with the promise of more (of the same—only bigger and better and brighter) to come. The victory in itself is not surprising since in this instance the American strong point was in contention against the Soviet weak point: the field of commercial advertising. In the field of political advertising this predominance is reversed, the advantage lying clearly with the Soviets.

For this same reason, incidentally, the Americans have so much difficulty mounting and maintaining (except for short periods of time, as in the case of the Moscow Olympics) a boycott. A boycott is an antieconomic measure; it is a political measure that seeks to counter natural economic forces. And it is doubly difficult for a commercial power to impose (see the rebellion of the American farmers against the attempted sanctions prohibiting the sale of grain to the Soviet Union).

On the other hand, the various uprisings that have taken place periodically among the Soviet Union's East European satellites have had more or less directly to do with the failure of the Communist system to satisfy the consumer needs of the populations concerned, most particularly the needs of the workers. This was true on June 17, 1953, when the construction workers of East Berlin began the demonstrations accompanied by violence that spread like wildfire throughout the country. It was true in Poland in 1956, 1968, 1970, and from 1979 to date. And it was true in Czechoslovakia from 1964 to 1968. It was, above all, the case in the Hungarian Revolution in 1956. (It is indeed odd that only in Communist countries have there been workers' uprisings since World War II.)

The fact that nothing comparable has happened in the Soviet Union itself is significant of the gulf that divides it from its "allies" to the west. But the gulf is gradually narrowing. The story of Solidarity has not been lost on the Byelorussians and, even more particularly, on the Ukrainians. Moreover, it has forced the Soviets to take a new look at the role of the so-called trade unions in the USSR itself.

Until 1981 "trade unions" in the Soviet Union acted as the "transmission belt" for orders, directives, admonitions, and cajolements from the party to the collective. Another, comparatively minor function was the arrangement of vacations and sick leave. Thus Soviet "trade unions" were in actuality the exact opposites of their namesakes in the conventional Western democracies. They have played a downright sinister role in the exhortation and exaction of increased production at constant wages which, of course, is tantamount to a cut in salary.

Especially conspicuous (above all, in Eastern Europe and the Soviet Union, where the official accent is always on espionage and sabotage) is the affectation of surplus American army uniforms, chevrons, insignia, and paraphernalia in combination with other American lay cultural articles of dress, such as the inevitable blue jeans, in a sort of uniform à choix. In 1983 the newspaper *Sovietskaya Rossiya* (Soviet Russia) published an article concerning the indignation of senior KGB officers over their observation that some junior officers of that organization appeared for work wearing blue jeans.

On May 22, 1984, *Pravda* published a "fierce clash of views" on Western fashions and rock music, revealing a profound generation gap—the oldsters calling for a strict ban and youngsters telling them to shut up. The newspaper reportedly received huge numbers of letters concerning an article the previous October which chastised people for wearing Western jeans and U.S. flags on their shirts and listening to "decadent" Western pop groups. Many writers called it a disgrace that people should wear American emblems when Washington was *the* ideological foe. Wrote a university lecturer: "We must not allow the Stars and Stripes into our lives at this time." Another letter writer condemned rock music as "something like a Colorado beetle, destroying all national culture around it."

According to *Pravda*, the youngsters replied with slogans such as "Hands off rock and roll," and one reader was cited as saying, "When you can make jeans better than Levi's, that will be the time to start talking about national pride." Most young people, said *Pravda*, were "incensed" at the idea that Western music and fashions should be banned. The newspaper went on to insist that they were indeed an evil influence and that ways should be found to combat them.

The infiltration and influence of American slang in all the major languages of the world and in many of the minor ones is a story that merits a book in itself. After almost forty years of occupation by the American and British armies it is hardly surprising that the German language (as spoken in West Germany, its largest home) is riddled with Americanisms. The word *clever* was quickly and unceremoniously adopted, so was *present* (for gift) and perhaps most significantly of all the word *Frust* was coined for *frustration,* having been preceded by *frustriert* (for *frustrated*). These words and many others have passed into the mainstream of the German vernacular. They are not cult objects.

In the Soviet Union myriad youth groups have seized upon American slang and buzz words, particularly *high life,* in terms like *khi-leifisti* (high lifers), and *swinger.* A practice which has enraged Soviet party hacks is that of writing Russian words in announcements, invitations, appeals, etc. in Latin letters. This is perhaps especially galling because Russian wire services and news agencies are obliged to telegraph their copy in Latin script; there is no international facility for the reproduction and reception of Cyrillic. (After World War II the Soviets resisted stoutly for a few years the use of English as the international lingua franca for communications—predominantly in aviation.)

When one compares this deluge with the very meager showing of the Soviet Union (the word *sputnik* from the Soviet space first and the single, solitary song "Moscow Evenings"), the striking imbalance between the two superpowers in the production of popular—not to say, pop—art becomes clear. In the field of literature the Soviets have one writer who wrote one book that was universally acclaimed: Sholokhov's *And Quiet Flows the Don.* On the other hand, the Soviet Union has inadvertently produced what, for its own purposes, is a negative, condemnatory elite in the corps of dissident writers and other artists who reject communism either as a whole or as practiced in the Soviet Union.

It is hard to say which of the two aspects of the opposing systems is the more striking: the sterility of the Soviet Union precisely in the field in which it is supposed to be most fruitful or the profusive fecundity of America where ideologically it was condemned to be barren. But it is only logical that the furious wowserism of the Soviet system should stunt the growth of art and only natural that "Utopia now!" should produce a great deal of good lowbrow entertainment—indeed, the best entertainment, and not all of it is lowbrow: Utopia is utopia.

But at what price? What price utopia? There have to be the paradigms, the shining examples of how the local boy can make it, the success stories that advertise the advantages of the system. Hence the million-dollar and multimillion-dollar contracts for football, basketball, and baseball players and the $10 million gates (thanks to national and international television hookups) for heavyweight boxing championship bouts. Hence the golden records that symbolize the sale of a million copies ("million" is the magic number in America. "When I want a million dollars," says Larry Holmes, "I go to the bank and get it." America has a million millionaires).

At what cost? There is, of course, the cost implicit in the tremendous wastage of a system of random rewards for success or what may pass for success—the money that simply goes down the drain. "An unspent dollar," said Andrew Carnegie, "is a stinking fish." Then there is the cost of neglect—benign or otherwise. Perhaps one-tenth of the nation suffers from chronic poverty. Here one must quickly add "by American standards." Poverty by American standards is not like poverty by European standards or Mediterranean standards, let alone African standards. "Genuine poverty," wrote H. L. Mencken, "is very rare in the United States, and actual hardship is almost unknown. There are times when the proletariat is short of phonograph records, silk shirts and movie tickets, but there are very few times when it is short of nourishment."

Times have changed somewhat. But it is still difficult to pin down "genuine poverty," to judge from Michael Harrington's comparatively recent book on the subject and the short flurry in the American press when poverty became a political football in late 1983. Still, regardless of whether "genuine poverty" exists, the contrast between rich and poor in America remains more than glaring enough.

The fatal paradox of the American dream, if there is one, is that freedom for all inevitably means the neglect of some. And in a population the size of that of the United Staes "some" is many. The hitch is that even Americans can't have it both ways. The great freedom Americans enjoy entails a categorical indifference to the lot of the little fellow, the unequally endowed by nature, the misfit.

American society is the society of "great expectations" in more ways than one. It turns on the expectation that every man will somehow be able to take care of himself ("rugged individualism") and perhaps a few others as well. The central idea of freedom blocks the imposition of a standard creed to live by and a basic minimum of training in a profession or craft that will enable the trainee to qualify as a wage earner. The fact that it offers such training and the opportunity to acquire such a creed is not enough. An offer of any kind is always a matter of degree. To be an offer convincing enough to qualify as a political measure, it would cease to be an offer and become an imposition.

What does it mean to give a man or a woman a chance? Is it enough to leave him or her unregimented to his or her own devices? Is such a thing feasible in any society, particularly in a highly commercialized society? The "naked square" sociologists talk about is not naked, but cluttered with junk. Is not, in fact, the unregimented, unmanipulated, uneducated, untutored, unskilled, barely literate, or only half-literate mass man the ideal butt or target of the advertiser, a creature who lives only for the moment and in the moment, the permanent resident of the "Utopia now!" of commercial advertising? If he is poor, he buys junk and lives with it. If he is rich, he buys junk again and again, keeping himself in new junk. The not-so-new junk that has to make way for the brand-new junk ends up in storage crates in warehouses. The ultimate repository of the "treasures" of the mass man is not the museum but the storage house.

The lack of discipline to acquire a discipline—that is, a trade, a craft, or the makings of a profession in an age of increasing specialization—is most telling not only among the disadvantaged strata of newcomers, especially illegal aliens, but also among the "traditional poor": blacks, Hispanics, and Indians who inherit and bequeath poverty from generation to generation. This phenomenon of an apparently irradicable, irreducible mass minority of permanently disadvantaged whom the new technology tends to lock out of the American system tends to frustrate and infuriate intellectuals in the United States and in the Western world at large. It is in itself a denial of the "upward movement" that is supposed to characterize democratic society and to recommend the system of free enterprise to the Third World as a model for economic development and social justice.

The essential nature of a democracy and its instinct for self-presentation are not such as to appeal automatically to poverty-stricken masses only just emerging from the colonial yoke, the "colonial yoke" being one of the most effective coinages of revolutionary romanticism. Nor have the recent huge trade deficits vis-à-vis Western nations and multibillion-dollar debts to Western private banks (backed by their governments) done anything to offset the Third World's inborn suspicion of its "capitalist oppressors."

It was therefore virtually preordained that the United Nations Educational Scientific and Cultural Organization (UNESCO) should become the effective international arm of the Third World (since most of the nations of the globe, particularly the new nations, belong to the have-nots). It was likewise easily foreseeable that UNESCO would take the field, campaign against, and clash with the United States of America as the leader of the free world and archpractitioner of free enterprise. Like its parent organization, UNESCO gradually came under the influence of the Soviet Union via the emerging African and Near Eastern states.

This was not an achievement of Soviet diplomacy so much as a windfall of history. The Arab and other Moslem states of the Middle East and Africa were locked in alignment against America's ally and protégé Israel, while the African states proper were just as unswervingly opposed to white South Africa. While South Africa was no longer an American ally (it had been in World War II), it remained geopolitically important to the West and staunchly anti-Communist.

Thus the die was cast in the colonial conquests and policies of the Western European nations of the previous century. No conceivable remedial action could have changed the outcome. The anti-Americanism of the Third World was, moreover, as natural as the basic alliance of the have-nots against the haves. The fact that the UNESCO machinery could be used against American interests at American expense (one-quarter of the budget of the organization was contributed by the United States) was *piquant* but no more than that, and the Americans finally wearied of it. They gave a year's notice of their withdrawal at the end of 1983 unless major reforms were enacted and their results demonstrated before that time. But regardless of whether the Americans stay or leave, UNESCO will never be the same.

Chapter XIV

What will be the same, what is bound to continue, whether the United States opts in or out of UNESCO, is the life-and-death struggle of the totalitarian and authoritarian countries to control the media. Of course, the only way to do this is on an international basis. Here the cudgels were taken up by UNESCO in its attempts to project and promote a "new information order." The issue was debated with more than a little exasperation in a 1981 UNESCO conference in Kuala Lumpur, in which Malaysia's prime minister attacked the Western news media. "It is because the exercise of the free press is so loaded in favor of the developed countries," he said, "that we have to fight for a new order. UNESCO is very well aware of this. All the principles of the UN were written by developed countries before the developing countries were admitted as members. Now...some of the loaded principles should be reviewed."

This was very much in keeping with UNESCO's 1978

mass media declaration, the 1980 UNESCO resolution
accepting the McBride report on the international press,
and the 1982 UN resolution banning direct broadcast
satellites. In September 1983 UNESCO with the UN
proper arranged a conference at Innsbruck. One of
the speakers, Wolfgang Kleinwachter (literally "small
watchman"—*nomen est omen*), gave a paper with the
title "Conceptualization of a New International Information Order: Perspectives of Discussions."

As described by Leonard R. Sussman in the magazine *Freedom at Issue*, Kleinwachter's central thesis
was the "autonomous province" that communications
have already assumed in international relations.
Against the background of the "fierceness" of the ideological struggle, Kleinwachter describes this autonomous province as "a global problem of mankind, a
challenge," the tackling of which "admits no further
delay." He argues that it is time to examine the international legal foundation for installing a "new order."
Sussman cites a Soviet authority to explain this: "to
establish international norms which would make it a
duty for states to tolerate no propaganda of certain specified conceptions and to make us, in the international
ideological struggle, only of such means as are admissible under international law."

Over the last several years the debates in UNESCO,
the UN Committee on Information, and the Political
Committee have produced a corpus of relevant documents. In his paper Kleinwachter accordingly concludes: "It emerges from these documents that
international mass-media activities may only take place
in conformity with the basic principles of international
laws," which he paraphrases: "Prohibition of the propaganda of force, the right of each nation to determine
its own national information system, the equal sovereign right of every state to participate in international
information relations, and the prohibition of information interference in the affairs of other states."

Such a statist basis, as Sussman points out, would
allow for no international news flow apart from government control. It would restrict the flow of news and

information to the people of the world to the minimum allowed by the most restrictive government as noninterference in its internal affairs.

Kleinwachter cites the International Convention on Civil and Political Rights, which assigns "special duties and special responsibilities" to the free dissemination of information. Then comes the hooker. Information rights, Kleinwachter asserts, can be implemented only in conjunction with other rights, such as the right to work. So the state must guarantee economic and social foundations as "a precondition for the dissemination of information." (This being so, what happens, one wonders, when the state cannot guarantee economic and social foundations? Here the context throws light on the pivotal significance of the Soviet Union's systemic economic failure.)

Perhaps the key restriction that Kleinwachter would impose comes under the heading of responsibility. Here the state's public media must comply with the demand to change their content "if another state looks upon such actions as interference in internal affairs." This would seem to conflict with the right, already mentioned, of such nation to determine its own national information system. But it does demonstrate the Soviet attempt, which is as remarkable as it is dogged, to impose its censorship on foreign states—including the United States—by logical extension.

Concern over the "autonomous province" of communications in international relations is not restricted to outright totalitarian and authoritarian persuasions. All political parties in Europe are wary of commercial television because it represents the loss of government control over a medium which has an awesome potential for influencing the masses. It is axiomatic that the farther left of center the party, the greater its reluctance to relinquish control of communications media. In France, for example, this is represented as the refusal of any "adulteration" of the public service.

Telecommunications has long since become a big business with a dynamic all its own, each advance in communications technology being dictated by the inability of the prior system to cope with the volume of traffic which that system had itself created. For the last several years the weekly *Tele Journal* has listed the programs of France's four "tele-neighbors": Germany, Switzerland (the French cantons), Luxembourg, and Monte Carlo. This list will soon be augmented by "Tele-Milan" (Italy), "Tele-Andorra," "Tele-Spain," BBC Television, and Britain's ITV commercial channel. The great explosion of the industry will come with the introduction of the direct broadcasting satellite. Tele-Luxembourg has already invested more than a billion French francs in buying up the rights to several hundred old films for broadcast via Lux-Sat—its communications satellite, which will flood France, Germany, and the Low Countries with commercial television programs in the appropriate languages.

This was the argument of Georges Fillioud, French minister of communications, when he recently announced the advent—in September 1985—of a French commercial television channel (via a French satellite): "If neighboring countries use their satellites commercially we shall have no means of intervention—neither with regard to the programs they broadcast nor with regard to the volume and nature of the publicity, the suitability of which they themselves will be the sole judges. Thus we would risk...the dilution of our cultural identity and at the same time the loss of the French publicity market to various [foreign] appetites [sic]. And be without any control whatever."

The Federal Republic of Germany will introduce commercial television at about the same time. Soon thereafter Austria will be forced to follow for the same reasons. There is much of the smack of the sorcerer's apprentice about all this. And suppose the "autonomous province" should become a world empire? What then—George Orwell succeeded by Fred Astaire? The genius—good and bad—of commercial romanticism has been too little studied, particularly in its connection with mass media.

Chapter XV

Information on the state of the Soviet economy is doubly important: First, it gives us a means of measuring the extent to which the state of the economy is known outside the Soviet Union, and secondly, it provides the subtrahend to be deducted from the official illustration (claims) of Soviet "reality in its revolutionary development."

In its statistical yearbooks and other compilations of data concerning the economy, the Soviet government has always resorted to various shifts to the end of concealing the actual state of affairs and conditions. The reason for this deliberate and elaborate policy of concealment was the awareness on the part of the enlightened members of the Soviet leadership that Soviet "reality in its revolutionary development" was a far cry from the actual state of the USSR economically or otherwise.

There was, to be sure, the expectation that the need for such deception would disappear within a comparatively short historical period. It has not turned out that way. To the contrary, the need for concealment has increased.

Another incentive to deception was the imperative to hide the extent and intensity of the radical measures adopted in order to achieve the "Soviet miracle." Undoubtedly the most famous of the "incentives" provided by the Soviet authorities was the Stakhanovite system for the increase of production. A samizdat document describes the genesis of the system:

In 1935 the production of coal in the USSR fell sharply short of the demands made upon it by all branches of industry. The important coal field in the Don basin was going through a prolonged doldrum, the quota had not been fulfilled; there was a shortage of 500,000 miners. The Central Committee of the Party sat in council on how to raise the production in the coal fields. They came up with the idea of a "Stakhanovite Movement." In the night from the 30th to the 31st of August 1935 the pickman Alexei Stakhanov was lowered in the shaft of the "Central Irmino" in order to set a record for the cutting of coal with a hand pick. Until that date all miners had worked in the traditional manner: every pickman cut the coal from the face of the shaft, then cleared it away, reinforced the scaffolding to support the roof of the shaft, and then turned to cutting. In that night Alexei Stakhanov only cut coal; others assisted him in that they took care of the clearing and reinforcing of the shaft. In such circumstances, and in any case at the cost of tremendous physical exertion, Stakanov succeeded in cutting 102 tons of coal in five hours and forty-five minutes, or fourteen times the standard daily norm. This "incentive," organized at the behest of the Kremlin, was immediately denominated the "Stakhanovite Movement." In practical terms this meant that in all branches of industry, transport and agriculture productivity had to be increased exclusively by means of intensified labor in the "Stakhanovite" manner, that is at the rate of fourteen times the previous norm. There began, in very truth, the most merciless exploitation of the workers. Yes, and Stakhanov himself. What sort of honorarium did he receive for his performance as chief actor in this spectacular of productivity? Within a few months he was spared all physical labor. He was sent to study at the Academy of Industry in Moscow from 1936 to 1941, then he was appointed manager of a shaft, and later actually became a member of the Ministry of Mining, having already been decorated with various medals and awarded the title of Hero of Socialist Labor.

The leitmotiv of the Soviet economy as a whole is the concentration on all means on armaments and the armed forces, beginning with research and development and proceeding through priority procurement for the mass production of arms and accouterment of all kinds. In a very direct sense the *nomenklatura* (the new class of middle and senior civil servants and functionaries) belongs to the armed forces and is an integral part of them; both the armed forces and the formation and maintenance of the *nomenklatura* through conspicuous privilege are security measures.

This systematic concentration on a few priorities (*Schwerpunkt* technique) is the underlying reason for the Soviet economic dilemma. It has skewed the entire system of priorities from the beginning. It is responsible for the studied neglect of agriculture and everything that goes with it, including the development of an infrastructure essential to it—roadnet, roadbed, rolling stock, in short a well-developed and smoothly functioning transportation system. The pivotal industry between armaments and agriculture is the chemical industry. No country in the world is rich enough to force the development of armaments industries and agriculture at the same time.

From the outset the Soviet Union chose to force the production of armaments with two major results: the catastrophic neglect of agriculture and the creation of highly specialized heavy and precision industries, the latter a development that leaves its economy with a technological base too narrow to compete on the world market at rational cost. The overall result is a paradox: an industrial base that is large enough to attract a wide variety of demands on it but so distorted that it cannot possibly meet them.

The inability to meet an increasing number of demands of increasing volume over several decades has long since forced the creation of what is now called the second economy. The older name for this phenomenon is black market. The black market, or second economy, is both a drain on and a supplement to the economy proper. It now accounts for as much as 25 percent of the Soviet Union's turnover.

The classic Communist feature of a planned economy is a central planning system that over a basic period of five years rigidly shortcuts consumer interests and needs in favor of heavy industry. In addition to the most formidable mass of military hardware in the world, it has produced a vast backlog of unsalable products— poor quality across the board and a high incidence of rejects. At long last the Soviets have come to the end of the primitive *Schwerpunkt* technique; they can no longer concentrate on a few priorities with utter disregard for expense.

Various factors, moreover, have combined to exacerbate the dilemma. There is an unfavorable demographic trend that brings less and less new blood every year to the labor force. There is the exhaustion of abundant and cheap raw materials, the erratic and cumbersome development of energy resources, the lack of suitable infrastructure, particularly in transport, the lack of sufficient investment in modernization against a background of poorly maintained, long-outmoded plants.

Between 1965 and 1970 the gross national product (GNP) of the Soviet Union rose from 45.5 percent of that of the United States to 53.7 percent. In 1975 there was a rise of almost 5 percent (to 58.2) which proved to be a flash in the pan. The percentage then fell back to around 54 and has pretty much remained there since.

Likewise the figures for the USSR's per capita GNP compared in percentages with that of the United States: There was a jump of slightly more than 10 percent (35.3 to 45.5) between 1965 and 1970 and since then a leveling off between 46 and 47 percent. So there has been a gain of roughly 10 percent since Khrushchev made his threat to bury the United States in open economic competition in twenty years. But ominously for the Soviet Union there has been no gain and even a loss in the last ten years (a loss of almost 4 percent in gross national product and a loss of more than 2 percent in GNP per capita since 1975). It is indeed in the last ten years the great rude awakening for the Soviet utopians.

To be sure the five-year plans have not been met for the last twenty-five years, but only since 1975 has the percentage increase of Soviet economic capacity fallen from 7 to 2–3.

The longer the Soviet leaders delay a meaningful reform of the economy, the greater the role the second economy will play. It already accounts in most estimates for 20 to 25 percent of the entire turnover of the Soviet Union. Thus the Soviet leaders have the choice of giving up some of their control to regional managers or having that control taken away from them in the gradual but inexorable process as in the past by the black market. The second economy is the Soviet euphemism for the emergence of the black market as a major competitor of the state commercial system. Its existence means that the state has virtually lost control of the people's dispensation of their incomes.

The rise and self-assertion of the black market in the Soviet Union is one of the great unwritten stories of our time. The fact that the black market managed to assert itself in the face of the Soviet Union's imposition of the death penalty for economic crimes is a tribute to the dogged ingenuity and the "commercial depravity" (as the Soviets would view it) of mankind. The phenomenon begins with the most famous of all the unofficial Soviet slogans: "They [the government] pretend to pay us, and we pretend to work." The point here is that when the Soviets began tinkering with the traditional value systems of the human race, they did not know what they were doing. They had only the foggiest notions about how the concept of state property as a universal system would affect the propulation at large.

If "Property is theft," as Proudhon insisted, then what is the theft of property? If all—or practically all—property belongs to the state, then the ownership becomes anonymous. Neither appeal to nor theft from an anonymity (the state) has anything like the same meaning as when these actions concern a private person—however remote he or she may be from the actual running of the entity concerned.

Theft of state property for private consumption or for resale on the black market is the most widespread form of corruption in the Communist system. This kind of theft is practiced without compunction, and no social stigma whatever attaches to it. Indeed, employees often regard such theft as their good right, a sort of perquisite that goes with the job—especially if they happen to be employed in a butchershop or supermarket or other highly prized form of consumer outlet.

The entire concept of *blat* (under-the-table sale or purchase) is as old as the Soviet state itself, at once the blight and the boon of the economy. With it the state commercial system cannot function as it should; without it the state commercial system could not function at all.

There are fabulous, breathtaking stories of commercial corruption, from the lowest to the highest state-corporate level, indeed into the ministries and the Politburo itself. There were rumors and even official investigations of Leonid Brezhnev's immediate family while the leader was still alive. Both his daughter and his son were called to account, and a close friend, the circus manager known as Alexander the Gypsy, was arrested and sentenced to eight years' imprisonment for theft and black marketeering. While Yuri Andropov lay dying, Moscow was rife with rumors that he had been shot by Valodya Brezhnev in revenge for the insult that Andropov had inflicted on the Brezhnev family with the investigation.

Surely the most spectacular corruption scandal of the postwar years was that involving the deputy minister of fisheries (who paid with his life for the escapade), which was reminiscent of *The Lavender Hill Mob*. In 1976 a middling member of the *nomenklatura* bought a can of sardines in one of the special shops for his kind. He was astonished when he opened the can to discover caviar. Thus began an investigation that ultimately exposed a smuggling ring dealing predominantly in caviar and beginning (as far as we know) with the deputy minister of fisheries. Each of the cans containing caviar was indistinguishble from those containing (and advertising) sardines save for a special but inconspicuous sign on the label. Members of the ring employed in the various retail outlets were assigned to sort out and secure the cans containing caviar for special sale. One of the cans had gone unnoticed, was put up for general sale, and the counterfeit was discovered. There were several death sentences pronounced and carried out as a result. The story of the Soviet black market is a study of the primordial power of supply and demand.

Chapter XVI

Marx was a city boy, and so was Lenin. Agriculture, strangely, has always been the stepchild of communism. More than that, Communists have often flown in the face of reason in agricultural matters. Beginning with the betrayal of the peasants in the granting of land and the annihilation of the kulaks, or larger peasant landholders, the Soviet state has more or less fostered an active enmity between itself and "the others," as they are called—the *kolkhozniki*, the collective farmers, whose living and working conditions are very considerably worse than those of the Soviet industrial or office worker.

Short of changing their agricultural system (unlikely except for further liberalization of the private plots), the Soviets have but one recourse in their need: continued investment in agriculture on an ever-expanding scale for machinery, fertilizers, and insecticides. This must be done in order to compensate for the unfavorable resources, particularly climate, infertility, lack of rainfall, and short growing season. Brezhnev declared in 1965 that the limits of new soil resources (the virgin lands program) had been reached and from now on the task was to improve the existing land under cultivation through better cultivating practices and greater industrial inputs. Since the 1965 agricultural plenum when the Brezhnev program went into force, capital investment in agriculture has been steadily increased.

During the eighth five-year plan (1965–70) state investment grew by 48 percent over the previous plan; during the ninth, by 45 percent; during the tenth by 40 percent. The increase so far during the current five-year plan is 40 percent. At present the annual investment runs to some 33 billion rubles, or slightly more than 25 percent of the total annual investment budget. But the return on the investment has been disappointingly small, a fact that has strengthened the hands of those in the opposition in the Politiburo who favor retrenching.

Apart from capital investment in agriculture, the Soviets massively subsidize food products. In 1978, 33.6 billion rubles were paid to subsidize the retail price of meat, dairy products, and other commodities. (In 1983 the same subsidy amounted to 48 billion rubles.) For example, the retail price of a kilo of butter in the state retail network is 3.60 rubles while the cost of production is 5.80 rubles. In fact, the gaps in the food supply can be seen in the distribution of the subsidies: Of the total, 65 percent goes for meat and poultry products, 16 percent for dairy products, and only 2.6 percent for grains. Soviet food price supports are the largest in the world, exceeding any in the West, both in absolute quantity and in relation to national income.

Fertilizer input has more than doubled since the inauguration of the Brezhnev plan in 1965, a fact that demonstrates the close interchangeability of fertilizer production with the munitions and other chemical industries. In recent years the output has run behind the plan. Thus it appears unlikely that the final target of 143 million tons per annum production will be reached.

Moreover, the fertilizers offered to agriculture are not of the proper mix, a situation contributing to the less than optimal responses from the field.

But the problems in fertilizer production designated for agriculture go beyond plant construction setbacks and faulty mixes. The Soviets estimate that losses between the producing plant and the field amount to 10 to 12 percent of total production (the result of theft, faulty loading and unloading procedures, and deficient transport). They also report that they have only 44 percent of the mineral fertilizer storage facilities needed. Yet in no area servicing agriculture have the Soviets made a greater effort than here. Even so, their use of fertilizers is about 60 percent of that of the United States. The comparison is even less favorable when fertilizer use per acre sown to crops is calculated: The Soviet total sown area is approximately one-third larger than the American area under cultivation.

Nevertheless, this is the sector in which the Soviets have achieved their most impressive results. But to what purpose? Fertilizers in the Soviet Union have been set aside for the use of industrial crops (cotton, sugar beets). It was only recently—in the mid- and late seventies—that the vast grain areas began to be supplied with fertilizers. And the results? Soviet sources reveal that during the last five-year plan the use of fertilizer increased on the average by 52 percent annually, yet the grain output during that period increased only 8 percent annually.

The mechanization of agriculture in the Soviet Union is a saga unto itself. There are 10,000 jokes about Soviet farm machinery, not least of them the melodic "lament of the Kolkhoznik whose tractor has betrayed him." Indeed, the Soviets have always had a messianic worship of the tractor. In the direst days of 1919 Lenin voiced his famous slogan: "If we had 100,000 tractors now, the peasants would be for Communism!" Since the 1920s tractor production has been a key target in the industrialization drive, and the fact that it could be quickly and easily changed to tank and assault artillery production gave the industry its primary strategic position. In the United States, by contrast, the changeover from horse to tractor began immediately after World War I. The comparative situation today explains much of the dynamic differences between the power resources of the two countries.

There is an annual flow of 360,000 tractors into the Soviet farms (this amount just about makes up for the depreciation and scrappage of the tractor inventory each year). Agriculture in the United States is far more mechanized than in the Soviet Union. The USSR has less than half as many tractors and trucks on farms but about 90 percent as many grain combines as the United States. The comparison is even less favorable if it is based on land area per machine: In the Soviet Union there is one tractor for each 250 acres of crops; in the United States there is one tractor for each 66 acres.

If garden tractors were included, the gap in mechanization would be 20 percent greater. (Despite twenty years of public advocacy, minitractors are still not in mass production in the Soviet Union.) There has been a slippage of 8 percent in the rate of tractor deliveries to Soviet farms during the last two five-year plans, a development that points to the primacy of defense needs.

Soviet agriculture faces a steady, high scrapping rate of farm machinery. Every year the Soviet Union scraps 12 to 13 percent of its tractor fleet. This makes for an average life expectancy for Soviet tractors of about eight years. Out of the annual flow of 360,000 tractors more than 300,000 are discarded in the same period. This has wrought havoc with the perennial plans to increase the size of the tractor inventory. The scrapping rate has not decreased with time, according to Soviet economists, and it also applies to harvesters (also eight years' life expectancy) and other harvesting machinery.

A number of factors are responsible for this state of affairs. One is machine quality; another crucial (and chronic) issue is lack of spare parts. Both factors result in a larger than necessary machinery fleet to ensure an adequate number working in the fields, an adequacy achieved only at the cost of cannibalization of machinery for parts that are simply not available in the regular supply channels. Also, a primitive rural road system has led to a higher scrapping rate. During some periods of the growing season, tractors are used to perform trucking chores because of mud, quagmires, and the near nonexistence of roads.

In order to solve the problem of farm mechanization on a continuing basis—dealing with the annual harvest crisis in machinery (breakage, shortage of spare parts and fuel)—throughout the entire nation, the Kremlin set up an All-Union Crisis Staff. Part of the problem is that here, too, a subsidy system exists.

Specialists estimate that the subsidy on farm machinery is 10 percent of the sale price, but on spare parts the subsidy is 40 percent. There is a surcharge. Such a system, Soviet economists contend, encourages cannibalization rather than the repair of machinery.

The problem of irrigation in the Soviet Union is likewise enormous. In the USSR 80 percent of cropland is subject to regular shortages of moisture. Nothing could be more effective in those areas favored with good growing seasons than a radical expansion of the irrigation network. Actually the Soviets inherited an effective irrigation system from the Czarist regime; then, as now, it was mainly concentrated in Central Asia for the growing of cotton. But the black earth of European Russia, the Ukraine and Volga, would greatly benefit from irrigation.

Irrigation, however, is costly, highly technical, and demanding of experienced operators. As matters stand, only 6 percent of the cropland is irrigated (the comparable figure for Bulgaria is 28 percent), and that mainly for the production of cotton. In 1977, 6.9 billion rubles were expended on irrigation, drainage, and land reclamation projects. This was Brezhnev's program and a testimony to the fact that no new lands are available.

In this crucial sector for the increase of food production (compare here with India, the Philippines, and Mexico with their green revolutions based on hybrid grain varieties, irrigation, and fertilization; their respective food shortages have been surmounted) the Soviets have arrived late. In Western Europe and the United States, both of which have normal rainfall, irrigation is one of the main methods used to maximize crop production. But there is, of course, always the cost coefficient.

It looks as if the Soviet leadership has finally decided to go ahead with a controversial multibillion-dollar project to redirect some of the flow of the USSR's mighty northward-flowing rivers to irrigate the parched farmlands of Central Asia and Kazakhstan. In an interview published in *Izvestia* on June 22, 1984, the USSR's first deputy minister of land reclamation and water resources, P. Polad-Zade, said that such a redistribution of the nation's water resources was now "an absolutely essential measure." He added: "There is no other way of supplying the south's need for water."

The project is very controversial and has been under debate for decades. In fact, the idea of a Siberian canal was first suggested in the 1830s, to correct nature's "mistake" whereby many of Russia's greatest rivers flow northward to the Arctic rather than southward to the potentially fertile agricultural lands of southern Russia and Central Asia.

The project now under discussion consists of two separate schemes, one for southern European Russia and the other for Central Asia and Kazakhstan.

1. To provide water for the Central Asian republics, the Soviets plan to divert waters from the mighty Siberian River Ob and its major tributary, the Irtysh. They will be dammed, and their water pumped south to irrigate farmlands in Uzbekistan, Turkmenistan, Kirghizia, Tadzhikistan, and Kazakhstan. After the water has been used for irrigation, it will go to replenish the shrinking Aral Sea.

2. A similar but less ambitious project is already in preparation in the European part of the USSR. The European scheme is cheaper and more feasible than the Central Asia plan and will transfer water from lakes and rivers north of Moscow—the rivers Pechora, the Northern Dvina, and the Onega—to

flow "backward" to the Volga, the great southward-flowing river that sustains much of southern Russia. This water will also help to revive the Caspian and the Sea of Azov.

The scheme relating to European Russia received sanction in the food program adopted in May 1982. It is the plan to divert the Siberian rivers that is really causing the controversy. A powerful lobby for the project exists in Central Asia, where party and economic leaders claim that with proper irrigation, the Soviet crop yield could be drastically increased, ending the need for expensive and embarrassing grain purchases from the West. They see the project permitting industrial expansion in the republics of Central Asia and in Kazakhstan, too, which would help alleviate the pressure of rapid population growth by increasing employment opportunities.

The scheme has met, however, with unusually strong opposition. So high and unpredictable are its potential consequences that an unprecedented ecological debate broke out and was waged between the two lobbies in the pages of the Soviet press. Those opposing the scheme include distinguished writers, artists, historians, academicians, and scientists.

The opponents claim, first, that the river reversal might cause serious climatic changes. The scheme calls for reducing the flow of fresh water into the Arctic Ocean, raising its salinity and therefore, scientists believe, lowering its freezing point. This in turn could cause shrinkage of the polar ice cap and a change in the weather and prevailing winds of the whole Northern Hemisphere.

Moreover, the diversion of waters from the north to the south would involve flooding thousands of acres of farmland and great tracts of timber forests and would force the abandonment of thousands of villages where the last remaining practitioners of old Russian arts and handicrafts survive. Thousands of people would be displaced from their homes, and their ancient towns and villages would be destroyed forever. The scheme would also, scientists claim, wreck substantial parts of the USSR's fishing industry by denying salmon and other river-breeding species their freshwater spawning grounds.

The debate has, therefore, ecological, economic resource, and even nationalist connotations. Many influential and vocal groups in the Russian Republic are passionately opposed to the scheme. Groups in Central Asia and Kazakhstan are just as passionately for it, seeing in the project a chance for their republics at last to play an equal part in the Soviet Union's development and to cast off their role of "little brothers" to the Russian Republic.

Then there is the problem of the nonexistent rural road and its context. During the long-drawn-out harvest season there is massive movement overland in rural Russia, when grain is trucked to the railway elevators and storage places. All the trucks in a republic are mobilized, and at peak season tens of thousands of vehicles are brought in from other republics, some of them thousands of miles distant. For grain is not stored directly after the harvesting and on the farms, as in the United States and Canada, but is moved into state elevators. Stalin, according to Khrushchev, did not trust the farmers to store grain at once and locally rather than wait till the roads got better after winter and they could conveniently truck it into the grain centers. The evidence is that Stalin's successors agree with him, for they direct that elevators and storage facilities be built *off* the farms. This makes for a peaking of needs for machinery, labor, and trucking when the roads are quagmires. Thus grain and crop elevator construction lag far behind demand.

In Kazakhstan, in years of good harvests, there occurs what is known as *khleboboyasan* ("fear of grain"). It is a time of incredible pressures and inevitable failure to meet accumulated needs. The long winter, bad roads (or no roads), the large variety of crops needing storage—all demand adequate facilities to keep crops fit for usage. The plan has priority but is seldom fulfilled. The current five-year plan calls for 30 million tons of elevator capacity to be built, but at the present rate of construction only about 22 million will be completed.

Farm-to-market roads—familiar to the American scene since the 1930s—are nonexistent in the Soviet Union. During spring and autumn most farm roads become hardly passable except for horses. Apart from strategic roads in the center and along the periphery of the European part of the Soviet Union—military-oriented radials from the center outward—there remains an incredible backwardness in rural transportation. Even the tractor and machinery stations of collective farms have their responsiblity to "maintain" the existing dirt roads in the provinces.

If it took the United States fifty years to build its farm-to-market interstate road system, it seems plausible that it will take the Soviet Union at least half a century and probably more to duplicate such an achievement. At the 1978 agricultural plenum it was found that the transportation of farm produce on roads was in a critical state and that the losses in transport were impermissibly heavy. It was implied, but not expressly stated, that additional roads would help solve the problem. There are no indications that anything has been done about it meanwhile.

Where Marx, Lenin, and all their orthodox followers have proved least effective is, of course, in dealing with the human factor. With a labor force in agriculture of more than 34 million people and a cultivated area of 550 million acres (44 percent larger than that of the United States), management plays a paramount role, indicated by the Soviet insistence that only party members occupy leading positions at the farm. However, Soviet farm managers are not fully responsible for making economic decisions directly affecting the output and profit of the enterprises. Almost always they must respond to directives rather than make independent decisions.

The pricing and marketing of farm products—apart from the private plots—remains a function of the state rather than a function of consumer demand. On-farm decisions are made only in conformance with a voluminous catalogue of regulations. A conspicuous chasm separates management from the workers on the Soviet farm. The administration has little contact with the peasant beyond the formal director–employee relationship. And the peasant has no voice whatever in the daily decision making that is characteristic of agriculture.

Were the private plots not part of rural policy—for they provide the primary incentive for most collective farmers—the system would be even more inefficient than it is. Brezhnev himself, in his 1978 plenum speech, charged that "all too often mismanagement, irresponsibility and indifference" still exist on a wide scale in the socialized labor force of Soviet agriculture. And this after fifty years of socialization.

On balance, as a result of differences in national resources, climate, technology, history, and the organizational systems of production, it seems almost unfair to compare the agricultural productivity of the United States with that of the Soviet Union. An official study of some five years ago found that in the Soviet Union one farm worker feeds seven people, while in the United States his colleague feeds forty-six and that with a much higher-quality national diet.

In view of the dynamics of the two systems, it is altogether likely that the Soviet Union will continue to be a net importer of grain and food generally until the end of this century—at least. The long-range plan calls for one ton of grain per capita by 1990—below the United States level—but even that goal, given Soviet conditions, seems illusory. If measured against the population given by the Soviet census, Soviet agriculture would have to produce 265 million tons of grain per annum within the next six years. For the last five years Soviet total grain production has remained below the 200-million-ton mark—well below, ranging from 10 to 30 million tons below.

Except for the single year 1978 (with 237.4 million tons) Soviet grain totals have shown shortfalls against annual plan quotas ranging from 10 million to 60 million tons (almost one-third of the overall quota!). For the years 1981 and 1982 the Soviets withheld the statistics. The policy of withholding figures on grain production (among other items of produce) is also a matter of commercial acumen. The object of the exercise is to prevent a price rise on the international grain market. If the outlook is bad and the Soviets are forced to go onto the market (as they almost always do, the amount needed depending on how big the shortfall in grain production is), then the price will rise. Thus they suppress all meaningful information concerning agricultural prospects during the year. As far as the Soviets are concerned, this is a matter of national security; the grain outlook and the gold outlook, which also affects price, are in the same category.

As a result of the Polish uprising in 1971, the Soviet leadership realized that more attention would have to be paid to consumer demand. They sought to increase the production of commodities in short supply, particularly livestock. Russians, like Poles, are great meat and sausage eaters. They measure a meal not by bread but by meat. For the next decade the Soviet doubled their investment in agriculture across the board. But in all the annual economic reports released in January (they are usually laudatory) is the same recurring one-sentence paragraph: "In a number of consumer commodities, particularly meat, the demand is not being fully met." This has been going on—the same formula statement—for the last nineteen years.

Meanwhile, the Polish uprising recurred—with a vengeance. In 1979 Solidarity exploded on the international scene, and in spite of two years of martial law in Poland, the explosions continue, albeit underground. The Soviet leaders, desperate for improvement, finally made the most fundamental concession to private enterprise they have ever made: They removed, under certain circumstances, the upper limits on numbers of livestock that may be held by individual farmers. The liberalization of Soviet policy on private plots had finally begun.

The question is whether liberalization, finally begun, was not begun too late. The Model Charter of 1935 provided, for each owner of a private plot, "one cow, two calves, one sow with young or two sows with young when considered necessary by *kolkhoz* authorities, ten sheep and ten goats, an unlimited amount of poultry and rabbits, and twenty beehives." In the years that followed, especially toward the end of the Khrushchev administration, there was a tendency in the alterations of the statutes toward the reduction of these holdings. There was always a difference in the limits placed on livestock holdings for *sovkhoz* (state farm) workers and for *kolkhoz* (collective farm) workers. The limits were stricter on state farms. For most *kolkhoz* households the juridical limits on the size of the private plots were set at half a hectare (1.25 acres), while the size of the private plot was limited to 0.15 hectares (a little more than a third of an acre).

In a decree on January 18, 1981, the limit on private livestock holdings was lifted altogether for those farmers entering into a contractual agreement with the collective or state farm. This did not mean that the private farmer had broken away from state control. It merely legitimized the widespread, almost universal, but illegal practice of more than two decades in which the farms provide young breeding stock and poultry and feed and pasturing facilities in return for the farmers' undertaking to sell the *sovkhoz*'s meat and milk. These can then be counted toward fulfillment of production and procurement plans. The whole arrangement smacks of sharecropping with livestock.

One of the strangest aspects of this decree was its almost hesitant promulgation. To be sure, the agricultural daily *Rural Life* carried a front-page résumé, and Radio Moscow mentioned it briefly the day before it was in force. A short summary was carried by TASS the day after. But no details of the decree were ever mentioned in any central newspaper. This is curious in light of the fact that decrees of far lesser significance are usually spread over the pages of *Pravda* and *Izvestia* ad nauseam. There can be no question that there was opposition to the decree in the Politburo and the Central Committee. But it is also likely that the muted publicity

given the decree was due to an understandable reluctance on the part of the leadership to give fanfares to
a measure that might well prove to be too little too late
and thus draw attention to the need for more of the
same. In any case, that is what happened.

The most radical departure from the Communist line
in the history of Soviet agricultural policy managed to
maintain meat production at the previous level, but it
could do no more than that. The effect of this tremendous innovation was merely to offset the ravages of the
massive migration from the farm to the city of rural
youth. Still, the production figures for the private plots
have been spectacular: "With less than three percent
of the sown area, the private sector generates one-
quarter of total agricultural output." This is an across-
the-board estimate unexpressive of the fact that the
enterprise is somewhat of a joint venture since the collective farms provide young breeding stock, poultry,
feed, and pasturing facilities (for payment in kind or
otherwise, to be sure). Even so, the success of the private plots is striking, particularly in the production of
meat: More than 50 percent of the meat produced in
the Soviet Union comes from the private plots. Fruits
and vegetables account for more than 30 percent of the
total Soviet produce. Private-plot farmers specialize in
the raising of pigs over cattle because the turnover is
much quicker: Pigs are slaughterable within ten months
of birth; the commensurate period with cows is two
years.

Now that matters in agriculture have come to such
a pass, it is generally agreed that the only way out of
the dilemma is to expand the area limits of the private
plots. Only by this means can the exodus of youth from
the countryside be stopped or can the young people conceivably be enticed to return to the farm. But such a
step would likewise mean the dismantling of the *kolkhoz*,
or collective farm, system altogether.

The perennial agricultural disaster in the Soviet
Union is related in various ways to the health crisis,
perhaps the most curious phenomenon in Soviet society.

While the rest of the world enjoys steadily increasing longevity, evidence suggests that the health of the Soviet people has been deteriorating in recent years. This is in sharp contrast with the giant strides made by the USSR to improve its health service after the Second World War. It is also an unprecedented situation for a developed nation.

Chapter XVII

Life expectancy for Soviet citizens, both male and female, stopped rising in the early sixties, and by the end of the decade, death rates were heading up again for nearly every age-group. Infant mortality rates, which measure the death of children aged under one year, rose by more than one-third between 1970 and 1975 alone. Life expectancy in the USSR is now about the same as the average for Costa Rica, the Dominican Republic, Panama, Taiwan, and Trinidad. Those nations, however, are moving steadily upward. The USSR appears to be heading down.

Nick Eberstadt, a demographer at Harvard University, wrote in the *New York Review of Books* (February 19, 1981): "Measured by the health of its people, the Soviet Union is no longer a developed nation." Jean Claude Chesnais, director of the Paris-based National Institute of Demographic Studies, said in September 1983, "This drop is something with no historic parallel in time of peace."

In a report published in 1980, Christopher Davis of Birmingham University and Murray Feshbach of Georgetown University showed that infant mortality in the USSR had demonstrated a phenomenal and unprecedented rise in recent years. Using data released by the Soviet authorities, Davis and Feshbach found that the infant mortality rate had abruptly increased by 36 percent between the years 1971 and 1976, from 22.9 per thousand live births in 1971 to an estimated 31.1 per thousand in 1976. The increase means that 38,704 more infants died in 1976 than would have if the 1971 mortality rate had still obtained. Since 1975 the Soviet authorities have not reported their infant mortality rate, but Feshbach has estimated that it could be as high as 40 per thousand today.

This unprecedented rise took place at a time when infant mortality declined almost everywhere else in the world. (The U.S. rate is now about 12 per thousand live births.) The USSR is the first of the nations of the developed world to experience a sustained reversal of the normal downward trend in infant mortality.

However, it is not only infant mortality that is rising in the Soviet Union. Except for teenagers, every age-group in the USSR had higher death rates in 1975 (the last year in which the authorities published such figures) than in 1960. Contrary to the trends in most of the countries of the industrialized world, the mortality rate for Soviet citizens has been steadily rising since the mid-1960s, from a low of 6.9 deaths per thousand in 1964 to an estimated 10.3 in 1980.

The life expectancy of newborn males has fallen significantly since 1965, from 66 years to 63, and may be still declining. (Chesnais estimates that in 1980 it was 61.9 for males.) Life expectancy of females, after a period of gradual extension, has leveled off at 74. (Life expectancy in the United States in 1983 was 69.9 years for males and 77.8 for females, according to the *U.S. News & World Report* of December 19, 1983.) The disparity between male and female life expectancy at birth in the USSR—some 11.9 years—is exceeded in no other developed country.

Davis and Feshbach listed a number of possible contributory causes of the rise in infant mortality. These include a worsening of diet. Specifically, there has been a drop in the numbers of mothers who breast-feed their babies, accompanied by a shortage of quality infant formula. There is also the poor quality of the housing—in particular, overcrowding and low standards of sanitation. Then there is the breakup of the extended family and the high level of female participation in the work force, leading to greater reliance on institutional child care. This may have caused a deterioration in the quality of care children receive. There are, in addition, the increased rates of illegitimacy and divorce and, finally, increasing environmental pollution.

After examining each possible cause, Davis and Feshbach found that the available evidence was too imprecise and fragmentary for them to reach any conclusion on the exact role played by each factor in the increase in infant mortality. Soviet officials and demographers admit that there has been a rise in infant mortality but claim that it is to be explained by improved statistical reporting and by demographic changes. Davis and Feshbach dismiss both these explanations as inadequate. Instead, they suggest other explanations which they consider more likely (though not proved, because of the lack of adequate information).

One likely cause, in their opinion, is the heavy reliance placed in the USSR on abortion as virtually the only available means of contraception. Some 10 million abortions are performed in the Soviet Union annually—that is, between 2 and 3 for every live birth. The average Soviet woman may have as many as 6 abortions in her lifetime (this is twelve times the U.S. rate). The more abortions a woman has, however, the greater the chances of damage to her reproductive organs. This may cause premature delivery when she chooses to bear a child, and the danger that the child will die is thereby increased.

Davis and Feshbach consider it likely that rising rates of alcoholism and smoking among pregnant women play a significant role in the recent rise in infant mortality. Indeed, the rising rate of alcoholism in the Soviet Union is the single cause most often cited as contributing to the overall mortality rise. The main cause of death in the USSR is heart disease, often brought on by alcohol and nicotine use. Heart disease has risen to epidemic proportions among Soviet citizens in the last twenty years, who have seen a 100 percent rise in such deaths, while the United States has registered a 15 percent fall in the same period. Half of all Soviet hospital beds in 1978 were occupied by patients with alcohol-related diseases, and alcohol is blamed for more than half of all fatal accidents in the USSR.

The U.S. Census Bureau reports, for example, that the death rate for alcohol poisoning in the USSR is eighty-eight times higher than in America. According to the 1982 study by Vladimir Treml of Duke University, per capita alcohol consumption in the Soviet Union has more than doubled, to about 16 quarts per year currently, from 7.5 quarts in 1955. Treml points out, too, that 60 percent of the alcohol drunk in the USSR is consumed in the form of hard liquor, which is more detrimental to health than beer or wine. He estimates that the Soviet Union's per capita intake of hard liquor in the early 1970s was more than twice as high as America's or Sweden's.

Some observers interpret these findings as evidence that the Soviet Union is undergoing a devastating health crisis. Eberstadt, for example, writes that it is extremely unlikely that "a progressive decline in the health of an entire nation, affecting people of nearly every ethnic background and nearly every age group," could take place unless there had been "a breakdown in the medical system." He believes, therefore, that the quality of medical care in the Soviet Union is actually declining. Davis and Feshbach, on the other hand, take a more cautious view. They write: "The quality of Soviet medicine in general has probably not deteriorated. But the 'extensive' development strategy followed in the health sector (more doctors, more hospital beds, etc.) has not improved the care for pregnant women and infants sufficiently to cope with the increasing threats to infant birth (abortion, smoking, alcoholism, growing environmental pollution, frequent epidemics of influenza)."

They sum up their conclusions: "...while it is apparent that medical facilities for pregnant women and infants have increased during the seventies as in previous years, the quality of care has not improved sufficiently to offset the increasing threats to their health from factors in the general environment."

Chapter XVIII

In the spring of 1983 there appeared a thirty-eight-page paper written by A. T. Zaslavskaya, a member of the Academy of Sciences for the Study of the Economy in Novosibirsk. The paper was allegedly leaked to a Western correspondent, but its nature was such that it could have been only a short time before its contents would have become generally known in any case. It stated in set terms what everyone at all concerned with the Soviet economy knows to be true. Beginning with the fact that in the last twelve to fifteen years the "economic development of the USSR has exhibited a tendency toward a perceptible decline in the growth rates for national income" (from 7.5 percent to 2.5 percent), the paper examines the causes of this decline and quickly concludes that the "state management of the economy" (exhibiting a "high degree of centralization of... decision making") is fundamentally, qualitatively, and generally unable "to insure complete and efficient enough utilization of the working and intellectual potential of society."

The original (and still prevailing) system was intended for a "comparatively low level of development of working people" and "proves to be incapable of regulating the behavior of workers who are more advanced in individual attitude and economically free" (Soviet workers change jobs frequently and now have more than 200 billion rubles in savings banks—a considerable problem in itself; they have nothing to spend their money on). Obviously "the existing system of production relations has fallen considerably behind the level of development of production forces." And this at a time when the imperative need to change the economy over "from an extensive to an intensive path of development can be done only by making use of all existing social reserves, of all the creative potential of the workers."

Then the blow falls. "The posing of these problems," continues Zaslavskaya, "presupposes a profound restructuring of state economic management, that is, specifically the abandonment of administrative methods with a high degree of centralized decision-making and the consistent comprehensive transition to economic methods of production regulation."

This is clearly a call for a market economy. It is a question, therefore, of the very existence of the Communist system. It is now more than twenty years since Nikita Khrushchev promised and threatened to "bury" us, confidently predicting that the Soviet gross national product would be greater than that of the United States by 1980. Instead, the general public is presented with a catalogue of the multifarious ills that afflict the Soviet body economic, sociological, and politic, as it turns out, chronically. The catalogue has been public for almost twenty years, having been the cause for the "major" economic reform under Leonid Brezhnev in 1965.

The Brezhnev reform accomplished nothing; it was a Band-Aid and mustard-plaster treatment when major surgery was urgently needed. (It did set the style for economic reform, including Andropov's "reform" calling for increased worker and managerial discipline and greater general effort.) The situation has steadily and drastically worsened over the intervening twenty years.

Corrective measures that might have proved adequate then are by no means adequate now. The huge investments in agriculture from the mid-seventies on were, and are, according to experts, exactly half enough and hence "not half enough" to produce reasonable returns.

Worse still, there is now a historical factor hard at work: The Soviet Union is at present undergoing a "demographic squeeze" of colossal proportions. In the sixties there was a growth birthrate of 17.8 per thousand; in the eighties it has already fallen to 8 per thousand. In the seventies 24 million workers entered the production process; in the eighties it will have been hardly more than 6 million.

At the same time—and this is the crowning irony—the Soviet Union supports a very large army of "hidden unemployed." Communist doctrine demands that full employment be secured at all times and at all costs. This exaction is one of the chief factors in the confusion of concepts omnipresent in the Soviet Union. Many—far too many—Soviet enterprises work at a loss. In a capitalist society they would declare bankruptcy or be written off. In the Soviet Union this cannot be done because the enterprise provides employment. (Something rather like this consideration has crept into the counsels of nationalized firms in the West: A firm is maintained at a loss because it is still cheaper than paying unemployment insurance.) In the Soviet Union the percentage of the labor force in "nonproductive branches" of industry continues to grow. In the seventies it was 11.7 percent; in 1981 it was 26.7 percent.

There is another debt that has increased by inexorable accumulation and must now be dealt with: the general obsolescence of plants in all branches of industry: metallurgy, mining, refining, the electro industry, transport.

There is, however, one whopping success story in the saga of Soviet industrial production, where the self-imposed and inherent disadvantages of the system have been turned to effective account for the Soviet Union—and this especially in the highly competitive field of international trade. This is shipping. Since the war, in

GEORGE BAILEY

addition to building up their navy to a point where it is second only to that of the United States, the Soviets have expanded their merchant marine spectacularly. The Soviet merchant fleet is now numerically the world's largest (7,500 ships).

In tonnage the Soviet merchant marine has grown from fourteenth in world rank in 1960 to sixth, increasing its volume six times and surpassing the United States fleet in the process. Of its ships 90 percent are less than twenty years old (compared with 60 percent for the United States). In composition the Soviet fleet includes transport ships, general cargo freighters, a deep-sea fishing fleet par excellence, and other specialized craft and a very large number of passenger ships.

The red flag is shown by more than sixty commerical lines servicing more than 120 countries. Of course, it was easy to discover the most lucrative traffic lanes for freight shipping: They run between the industrial centers of Western Europe, North America, and the Far East. Within a few years the Soviet merchant fleet cut a swath of extraordinary proportions through what had been the preserve of Western private enterprise. At one period Soviet lines were carrying 13 percent of the general cargo between the American East Coast and Western Europe and at least 25 percent of the goods traffic between America and Germany.

In the area between the American West Coast and the Far East, the Soviets' Vladivostok-based Far East Shipping Company (FESCO) has become the most successful in a field of twenty-four competing firms, and this by a margin of 23 percent over its nearest competitor. The Soviets have been just as spectacularly successful along the shipping routes between Europe and East Asia, likewise a traditional domain of Western carriers.

The Soviets achieved these remarkable results in a comparatively short time by the simple device of undercutting their competition at every turn. They operate as independents, unbound by any of the conventions and rates laid down by the liner conferences of their competitors. FESCO, for example, succeeded in dominating the Pacific carrier trade by offering "dumping" rates as much as 38 percent lower than the rates of conference members! In effect the Soviets, using their advantage as a company owned by a state that plays the game under a wholly different set of rules from those of its rivals, have waged a continuing price war against the established shipping firms of the world.

While it is not accurate to say that a financial loss is a matter of indifference to the Soviets, they are indeed willing to accept such losses in order to gain a political (or a military) point or in order to secure a hard-currency income. And who is to say what it is worth to them and in which terms? There are, of course, situations in which Soviet reasoning is perfectly clear, as in the drive for northbound cargo from East Africa to Europe: Soviet ships were carrying supplies to Mozambique, much of it guns and ammunition, particularly during the long period of guerrilla warfare in Zimbabwe. Why make the long voyage home in an empty ship?

Similarly, much, if not the major part, of the Soviet shipping rationale is strategic, meant to serve directly or indirectly as support for ongoing or projected military operations. The huge Soviet deep-sea fishing fleet is equipped with electronic equipment far in excess of any conceivable nonmilitary need. As noted earlier, the Soviets believe in espionage as much as they believe in logistics. Espionage is the obverse side of their communications policy. Moreover, it complements the credo of Mikhail Frunze: "In a modern state it will be necessary to achieve the complete militarization of the entire civilian economy." The fact that the Soviets have decided as a matter of policy to carry an increasing proportion of trade between non-Russian countries is in keeping with Frunze's dictum.

It is also expansionist. The Soviet Union is not a great trading nation. The Soviets make no contributions in banking or insurance skills or technology in the voluminous exchange of goods between Japan and Western Europe. Yet they now carry 25 percent of all Japanese exports to Europe. The Soviet passenger ship fleet can boast equally spectacular successes. Admiral Sergei Gorshkov summed up the overall effort on Soviet Navy Day in 1976: "Maritime transportation, fishing, and scientific research on the sea are part of the Soviet Union's naval might."

Has the Soviet seagoing navy caught up with the navies of the West? Well, yes and no. Here is an excerpt from an article in the August 1976 issue of the Soviet magazine *Iunost'* (*Youth*):

In order to heat the force pump it is necessary to place a torch [a wad of waxed cotton at the end of a stick or rod] in an air current full of uncondensed gasoline. In order to ignite the torch it is necessary to light a match. But matches, especially when one is in a hurry, have a habit of breaking. So the officer of the fifth unit [the electromechanical battle unit] would take a box of matches from the stoker, take out a match, strike it and protect the feeble flame in the palms of his hands. The air pumps begin to shriek and the two force pumps groan through the rocket-launching tubes....

What is being described here is the firing of the boilers of a modern Soviet cruiser (battleship) in answer to the command "Prepare ship for battle and immediate engagement." But the idea of a stick, a wad of waxed cotton, matches—all these antediluvian props where, on a comparable American battleship, let us say, it would be a matter of pressing a button.

But perhaps this whole procedure of heating the force pumps of a Soviet cruiser is an exception, not the rule? Perhaps the remaining mechanisms of the B CH-5-class cruiser are in keeping with the technical development of the epoch of nuclear energy and rocketry? Not at all. The author of the magazine article describes how the crew makes its way through the corridors, shafts, cisterns, and interstices of the cruiser exactly as if they were in the circles of Dante's hell—officers, mates, and sailors detecting and removing fissures, cracks, and warpings one after the other, from a broken magistral line of the system of steam fittings to the burned-out ball bearings of the pistons.

And it's easy to say "detecting" because in this area, too, there is a very considerable backlog: Soviet ship-builders are constrained to go all out for quantity and thus have very little time to think of increasing the quality of anything they do. So it happens that the fissure and cracks in pipelines have to be detected by hand—running the tips of the fingers along the whole length of the magistral line testing for hot and cold.

How different, ventures the Radio Liberty commentator, himself a former Soviet naval officer, from the American cruiser *Long Beach* which he visited not long ago. There in the electromechanical battle unit is a control station with a huge, many-sectioned light-studded panel running the length and height of the whole wall. Press a button, and you get a colored light illustration of the entire system of steam pipes; press another button, and there lights up before you a picture of the ship's lubrication system; press yet another button, and you are shown the ventilation system. If a fault develops in any one of the systems, a buzzer sounds and an electric rabbit runs along the panel to the trouble spot requiring repair. And the repair work itself is done in a way that is nothing like what happens on a Soviet ship where every tooth in a sprocket has to be changed. On the American ship an entire block of equipment is removed and replaced, the actual repair work being subsequently done by specialists onshore.

One of the most interesting phenomena of the Soviet command economy is the *tolkach* (pestle or pounder), a scrounger who goes outside channels in order to procure material or equipment in critical need or otherwise resorts to unorthodox ways and means to get things done. Every factory director has his *tolkach*, just as every senior military commander in every army in the world has an officer entrusted with such duties (here again the military usage is the model).

It is obvious that the *tolkach* is essential to the Soviet system. Without him the economy could not function. It is equally obvious that the *tolkach* is something like a semiofficial black marketeer, empowered to get what is needed by hook or crook. It is not so obvious that his involvement in economic criminality is only a matter of degree and that the more successful he is, the greater the degree of his involvement. The annual average of those sentenced to death and executed (the sentences are never commuted) for economic crimes in the Soviet Union is 300. The high incidence of *tolkachi* in this dismal statistic is well known in the Soviet Union but nowhere registered officially.

Considering the efforts and sacrifices made and the expectations aroused, the saga of the Soviet economy is the story of an almost unrelieved failure on a colossal scale, the consequences of which—in the nature of things—are simply untellable.

In terms of public relations the Soviet Union has suffered three catastrophes in the last twenty years and more: politically (it has been forced to intervene militarily on repeated occasions in order to maintain a manifestly unpopular political system among its satellites), culturally (it has failed to produce works or achieve performance standards commanding international recognition but, to the contrary, has incurred spectacular humiliations in the loss of its best artists and writers through defection), and economically (it has a steadily diminishing growth rate and perennially low standard of living). As a result, very few Third World countries have gone over to communism upon gaining their freedom.

Against this stands the equally spectacular increase in the quantity and quality of Soviet arms in both absolute and relative terms. In the last twenty years the Soviet Union has drawn abreast of the United States and its allies in nuclear arms and perhaps, in some respects, has surpassed them, meanwhile increasing its advantage in quantity of conventional arms.

Economically the picture is clear. The concentration on armaments played a key role in reducing the country's overall performance. Politically and culturally one might ponder whether the failures are the cause or the result of the concentration on the military. Culturally, at least, it seems often enough that the Soviet leaders have simply resigned themselves to mediocrity. If so, they have for once taken a realistic view.

There is also a demographic squeeze in the Soviet Union with hardly more than a quarter of the influx of seven years ago now entering the labor force. This contraction will last for at least another twelve to fifteen years. And while it will wreak havoc with the economy, another even more sensitive field in this respect is the armed forces, especially the army. The most publicized aspect of the demographic development in the Soviet Union to date has been the relative rise of the non-Slavic and largely Moslem sections of the population. In six years every fourth recruit in the Soviet Army will be a Moslem. By the year 2000 every third Soviet soldier will be a Moslem. This situation is bound to be a very large complicating factor in the army command structure. At present non-Slavic soldiers in the Soviet Army serve for the most part in service units. But with the higher percentages now looming this will no longer be possible.

In the last few years, largely as a result of the Soviet invasion of Afghanistan, the Soviet army has drawn some attention from the media. Another perhaps equally important factor is the so-called third wave of recent Soviet immigrants, many of them young enough to have served in both the Soviet and the Israeli or American (or other) armies and thus to draw comparisons. These are often striking. During his two years as a recruit in the Soviet Army, 1958 to 1960, Eduard Kuznetsov, the dissident writer, fired a gun only once. It was a Kalashnikov, and he fired five rounds, three in a "burst" and two singly. After his solo performance Kuznetsov was classified as a machine gunner automatic rifleman in the Soviet Army. In the Israeli Army Kuznetsov fired a variety of guns twice daily, using up from fifteen to twenty rounds on each occasion.

A Soviet officer (recruit) as recently as six years ago fired a Kalashnikov (thirty rounds) and his service pistol (ten to fifteen rounds) once a month. Officers in the Israeli Army fire a variety of weapons about twice as often as enlisted men. The emphasis on marksmanship is very strong throughout the Israeli Army, and contests with various weapons are frequent.

In an April 1984 issue of the Soviet Army newspaper *Krasnaya Zvezda* (*Red Star*) there appeared a detailed report of the insuperable difficulties with increasingly complicated modern weapons experienced not only by the rank and file (often with only rudimentary education) but also by the officers. Regimental commanders are confronted with the problem of providing troops with considerable supplementary technical instruction to the ordinary military training in order to service the necessary machines. The author of the article concludes that several years of technical instruction will be necessary in order to prepare troops properly.

"Instructions for use, directions for the storage, repair, maintenance and practical application are all too often neglected," so says the *Red Star*. The complicated instruments concerned are roughly and incorrectly used and soon ruined as a result. (In any given Soviet regiment—apart from elite units—at least half of the heavy machinery is out of use at any one moment.) *Red Star* goes on: "The consternating truth: in Poland and the GDR [German Democratic Republic] there are better soldiers than in the omnipotent Soviet Union because the educational standards are higher....The German soldier accepts these magnificent new weapons as a challenge to his ability to master things technical and make them serve him. The Russian acts in exactly the opposite way: he shakes his head and tries to forget about the complicated new machines as quickly as possible. The same thing goes for the instructors."

More than half the Soviet officer corps is made up of professional soldiers. But most of the noncoms and all the rank and file of Soviet soldiery are reservists. The unsatisfactory quality of reservists has been brought to light in some four years under the glaring sun of Afghanistan. Indeed, the Soviet Army in Afghanistan is like the U.S. Army in Vietnam—*mutatis mutandis*, but without the equipment, without the know-how, and without the constant exposure to the media.

Chapter XIX

As for the Soviet system of alliances, in the case of the Warsaw Pact the question is whether the "allies" are assets or liabilities. (One has only to remember that Warsaw is the capital of Poland; except for Bulgaria, the "allies" are liabilities.) But there is an automatic trip wire in the case of East Germany (just as there is in the case of West Germany for the West). If it is not axiomatic that neither Germany will fight the other Germany under any circumstances, it ought to be. The hostage status of East Germany in the Eastern bloc enforces the effective neutrality of West Germany between the two blocs. This is one of various reasons why NATO strategy is defensive while the credibility of the Soviet military threat (the only cement of the Eastern bloc) demands that Warsaw Pact strategy be offensive. Offensive capacity, unit for unit, is more expensive than defensive capacity. In this sense the overall strategic doctrine of the Soviet Union has forced its own hand, so to speak; it must keep plunging. It has been boxed in schematically by its own doing.

For something like the same reason—or complementary reasons—the United States is forced to pursue an overall defensive strategy. One of the aims of Soviet grand strategy is to maneuver or provoke the United States into taking military measures that its own and its allies' constituent publics will not accept or support. The burden is thus on the United States to prepare every step of the way with a public relations campaign designed to make such steps palatable to the general public. This necessity sets limits to the actions and reactions of the Americans. No such restraints are imposed on the actions of the Soviet, a fact that is by no means always an advantage to the Soviets. Their very freedom of action in this regard is a constant temptation to react massively, extravagantly, overexpensively. Likewise, the Americans can count themselves blessed for the restraints on spending that the power of public opinion places upon them. The thesis that restraints on spending are a blessing in disguise (the disguise is a good one) includes preordaining an American emphasis on the economic rather than on the military. Here, obviously, a balance must be kept.

But it is easier to keep a balance when economic considerations are predominant and restraints are public. It is not just that the Soviets have taken the offensive and the Americans the defensive in this confrontation. It is, rather, that the Soviets are, by design, predisposition, and force of habit, conducting a military struggle while the Americans, by both public constraint and natural predilection, conduct their part of the struggle far more along the lines of economic warfare.

In good part this is merely a matter of playing one's strong side and favoring or sparing one's weak side (this applies to both the Soviet Union and the United States). Cost accounting is an American strong point and a Soviet weak point (in the Soviet Union it is difficult to determine the real price of anything). Thus the American strategy does not exhaust itself over the success or failure of boycotts against the Soviet Union. It concentrates

rather in provoking the Soviet Union and its satellites
to overspend, to embark on ventures entailing tremendous and unnecessary expenditures, meanwhile taking
every precaution not only not to follow suit but to put
to use all the imagination and *savoir faire* of free enterprise in devising grand-scale economics within the
framework of strategic thinking. "A bigger bang for a
buck" has been much maligned as a harmful economy
in utter forgetfulness of the fact that it does represent
sound economic policy. Also, economics is perhaps the
only field in which Americans are prepared and even
accustomed to think in the long term.

Indeed, the Americans seem prepared to accept apparent military disarray, as at present in NATO, so
long as the economic situation is relatively stable. While
the European Economic Community is long established
and a power to be reckoned with, there is no such thing
(as noted earlier) as a European defense community.

In the same way SEATO is a loose alliance of a few
Southeast Asian states of no great military importance
within the vast American security area of the Pacific.
The most striking aspect of the overall arrangement in
the Pacific is that America bears almost the exclusive
responsibility for the security of the entire area (the
Japanese Self-Defense Forces are at best the nucleus
of an armed forces potential) in a formal allocation of
roles with its allies. On the other hand, the strategy
involved has been overshadowed and eclipsed by the
truly sensational emergence of Japan as the second most
powerful industrial state in the world (Japan moved
into second place ahead of the Soviet Union last year).

Probably the single most important event in the whole
of the Asian area since the Second World War was the
signing of the Sino-Japanese Trade Treaty in 1980. (Instead of occupying this place of preference with China,
the Soviet Union is to all intents and purposes completely out of it.)

It is not only Japan that has flourished economically.
South Korea, Taiwan, Hong Kong, Singapore, Thai-
land, and Malaysia have more or less followed suit. In
fact, the general economic success throughout the area

has been such that something like a major economic and geographic shift has taken place on the world scale.

Likewise, American overtures to China have been economic rather than military—for a number of good reasons. When Henry Kissinger opened the road to relations with China, he commented that the most important thing was to avoid giving the Soviet Union cause to become paranoid over increasing encirclement. While it is not consummately easy to find a casus belli in the signing of a technical or economic treaty between great powers, the Soviet Union left no doubt in the minds of the world public that it did not like the agreements between the United States and China signed during the visit in May 1984 of President Reagan. The point here is that while the military strategy of the United States vis-à-vis the Soviet Union is defensive, the economic strategy of the United States vis-à-vis the Soviet Union is anything but defensive.

For its part the Soviet Union has three client states in Southeast Asia: Vietnam, Laos, and Cambodia. But there is a war going on in the last of these and constant skirmishing and artillery duels going on between the People's Republic of China and the first of these. Moreover, none of these is anything like an economic asset to the Soviet Union. To the contrary, all three are definite liabilities. In military and strategic terms, of course, they are of considerable value. But they were purchased at the price of China's enmity, a loss they do not begin to compensate for.

There remains in the area only the pathetic case of North Korea. It lives in a form of international ostracism. In 1979 it reneged on a loan of $40 million to a Swiss bankers' consortium. Since then its credit has not been good. Apart from stigmatizing itself by its savagery along the international demarcation line between the two Koreas (and boorish attempts to bribe foreign diplomats), North Korea has managed to lose one-quarter of its population (5 million) through the attrition of a plummeting birthrate in the last thirty years. It now has a population of 15 million, compared with South Korea's 40 million. In the Sino-Soviet struggle North Korea has managed to remain neutral—apparently by assiduously cultivating its pariahdom. Most recently the country's megalomaniac leader, Kim Il Sung, having secured the succession of his son, has been reduced to begging for reunification as the only way out of the desperate general dilemma.

Militarily the Soviet Union's position in the Pacific area is not particularly good. Economically its position is all but disastrous. Nor are the prospects for stability in the area good: for one thing because of the rapid degeneration of North Korea; for another because of the continuing convulsions in Cambodia and the involvement in the struggle—along Vietnam's northern border—of the People's Republic of China.

Chapter XX

Nowhere does the United States' determination to price the Soviet Union out of the superpower confrontation gleam more brightly than in the heavens. In the last thirty years the Soviets have sent well over 1,000 of its cosmos series satellites (communications and "killer satellites") into orbit. The United States has for its part sent hardly more and probably less than 25 percent of that number of communications satellites into outer space during the same time.

The reason for this modest American showing was that the Americans, confident of their technical superiority after the moon shot, were content to allow the Soviets to shoot billions of rubles into space for the purpose of establishing a system of killer satellites and communications. Up to a point (a point the Soviets have not reached) the Americans felt they could take care of any rockets the Soviets might launch from land, air, sea, or space with a highly refined intercept system based for the most part on land and sea. The design and development of the Challenger sky lab shuttle program in which the same spacecraft can be used over and over again is another example of achieving an astronomical saving while scoring a space first. If possible, the Challenger program bothered the Soviets even more than the moon shot—not least because of the recurrent publicity that comes with repeated use of the same spacecraft.

A few days after Neil Armstrong had put his foot on the moon I chanced to meet an old acquaintance, a Soviet editor, in the Brussels airport. He was the picture of dejection. "What's the trouble?" I asked.

"Armstrong," he answered.

"Don't worry," I said, trying to console him, "It won't be long until you are on the moon, too."

"A lot you know," he answered. "It is not a matter of months with us. It is not even a matter of years—it is a matter of decades!"

Indeed, we are now halfway through the second decade since Armstrong put his foot down.

Nothing that Ronald Reagan has done has so alarmed the Soviets as his announcement of an American Star Wars program. The very name is full of computer magic (and computers are a branch of electronic science in which the Soviets lag well behind the Americans and fall farther behind with each day). If it were nothing than a publicity stunt, it would stand as a masterstroke in the international media war between the two superpowers.

But it is something else. The Strategic Defense Initiative, as the Pentagon calls the program, even in its first five-year phase, which calls for nothing more than an exploratory research effort, will cost $25 billion. Most dismaying of all for the Soviets, the program will commit the United States to a highly imaginative space odyssey over several decades. This is a double blow because the Soviets have always regarded space as their natural preserve (long before the first sputnik Soviet popular science books were full of the romanticism of space and the Communists' special place there) and because the program emphasizes the long term (the long term being heretofore another special Soviet advantage over the unhistorically minded Americans). This prospect, ironically, threw the presidential elections of 1984 into all the stronger relief. If Reagan failed to gain reelection, the Star Wars program could be stopped. It is pretty strictly the President's baby. But if Reagan were reelected, the program would be set in budgetary concrete during the four years of his second term, the size of the accrued investment itself meanwhile setting the future course of the program after Reagan had left the scene. The Soviets managed to surmount the tremendous psychological reverse involved in the moon shot because the Americans themselves in their fickle devotion to the here and now turned from the space effort like children tired of a not-so-new toy. The Star Wars program represents a permanent commitment on the grandest of all scales.

American advantage in the space race rests chiefly on the United States's superiority in computer development and refinement, particularly in the article of miniaturization. Computers play a determining role throughout the entire process of rocket and satellite payload development, even controlling the slopping of liquid fuels as well as adjusting and correcting the projectiles' course of flight. But the research and development of computers require a broad technical and industrial base the Soviets do not have and a freedom of individual initiative they refuse to grant. The refusal to grant the necessary freedom to the individual is on display in the Soviet government's decision not to market the microchip personal computer. To have done so would have broken the government's monopoly on communications. This the Soviets could not do without encompassing the doom of their system.

Chapter XXI

It is apparently generally conceded that the coming and development of the computer have changed American life more than any other single factor in the last quarter century. For one and perhaps the most important thing, computerization has meant breaking up huge industrial concentrations and spreading them far more equably over the landscape of America. This has accomplished a radical redistribution along geographical lines of both consumer and producer power, based on major shifts of population from one region to another.

The West, South, and Southwest have benefited (or suffered, as in the case of California) from huge influxes of people over a comparatively short time. It is extraordinary how quickly and in what masses people move in America. Also extraordinary among nations, but not for America, is the huge influx of immigrants, both legal and illegal; the United States is the only major country in the world with an unremitting mass im-immigration.

This in itself throughout American history has been a tremendous force for change and expansion, as the columnist Joseph Kraft has noted. He calls it "a kind of American yeast" and adds that experts regard the present flood of immigrants as comparable to the great waves of the late nineteenth century. America is willy-nilly a dynamic society that is becoming more and more diversified thanks to the miniaturization of computers.

Never before has commercial romanticism had such a fine, free field to romp in. In April 1984 a reporter attended the computer dealer and product show in Las Vegas. There were some 1,500 exhibits, almost all having to do with microcomputers. The reporter, Jerry Pournelle, predicts that "the micro revolution will transform society in ways more fundamental than ever did the automobile or television....Before the end of this century, big computers will be linked together in networks of staggering complexity. Microcomputers will give everyone access to these nets. By the year 2000 anyone in Western civilization who wants to will be able to get the answer to any question, as long as the answer is known or calculable."

It is easy to make such a prediction for America. The way is clear, unencumbered. As Arthur Schlesinger, Jr., put it in the magazine *Encounter* in September 1970, "Societies where power is distributed and diversified are more likely to retain the flexibility necessary to deal with the velocity of history." But what about the Soviet Union? How stands it with the Soviet ability to deal with the "velocity" of history? Can the Soviet Union devise a way to use computers without losing control over them? If it does, how will this affect its ability to compete with the United States and the West in general?

In the early stages of computer technology, when the accent was on large computers institutionally controlled and adaptable to centralized planning and command functions, the wind seemed to be blowing full blast in favor of the Soviet Union. But with the advent of the microcomputers and the personal computer the wind has shifted 180 degrees. The significance of the personal computer is that with it the private person has come into a position of power and influence unparalleled in history. In the United States the private person can buy an Apple computer or an IBM PC with internal memory and, if need be, connect it to larger mainframe computers by simply hooking it up with his telephone.

Every microcomputer or word processor is a potential printing press. It will print as many copies as one may want. In the Soviet Union private ownership or possession of printing presses or even photocopy machines is prohibited. When Solzhenitsyn visited Spain in 1975, he showed his Spanish host a document. "Ah," said the Spanish friend, "we must have that photocopied!" and took Solzhenitsyn to a public photocopy machine in a nearby store.

"Did you have these photocopy machines under Franco?" asked Solzhenitsyn.

"Of course," answered the Spaniard.

"Then," said Solzhenitsyn, "you don't know what dictatorship is."

In the chaotic, individualistic, wide-open, free-for-all marketplace of America, ideas and projects spring up overnight. In the twelve months before March 1984 in Silicon Valley some 100 new high-technology firms were established. In the United States the danger, as portrayed in the American film *War Games*, is that a private microcomputer operator will manage to hook into some central data bank system and draw from it and feed into it. In the Soviet Union the danger is that the central network of computers will not be able in all cases to monitor and control all microcomputers, recording all manuscripts and files as they are created. (Here again we have an example of the diametric opposition of the two systems: the danger of breaking in as opposed to the danger of breaking out.)

The Soviets are clearly in a quandary about this, but so far the pattern seems to be that of housing and controlling all computers institutionally. But if the Soviets decide definitively to regulate the use of computers, they will inevitably stunt the growth of the computer industry at large and curtail computer literacy among their youth. Moreover, they will have to forgo the mass production of computers, thus losing the advantage of economics of scale. In short, they will reduce the capacity of the country to compete internationally in the computer culture, particularly with the full-fledged "information societies" now forming in the industrial countries of the West and (perhaps more ominously for the Soviet Union) of the Far East. The Soviet Union is at various disadvantages both systemic and technical in trying to form a computer society. Its telephone system is so bad that attempts to hook computers to telephone lines have had to fall back on special lines or a "search" system to find lines good enough for high-speed communication. (Apparently only one out of every twenty or thirty lines will serve the purpose.)

In the mid-sixties I spent part of one summer in the Soviet Union trying to find a telephone book. I saw one in the Intourist office of the Hotel Moskva (it was kept in a locked desk drawer to which it was attached by a fairly heavy chain) and one in the American Embassy in Moscow. I never saw another. My search was a charade. Everywhere I went I asked after a telephone book. Sometimes surprise was feigned: "You mean to tell me we don't have telephone books? Well, well, well!" or "Now that you mention it—yes, we have no telephone books—I just never thought of it before!" Finally a young woman Intourist guide gave me an explanation: "We used to have telephone books—about fifteen years ago, I think. But then they discontinued them. Why? Well...too many people were calling too many people and saying nasty things to them."

The confrontation between the Soviet Union and the United States of America is an unequal struggle in every respect. Indeed, in some respects the struggle is so unequal that it is hardly a struggle at all but is rather the coexistence of two behemoths moving on parallel tracks, going by each other in opposite directions but never meeting. They are judged comparatively by the majority of those with any means of making themselves heard because of their size and power and the danger immanent (but not imminent) in the confrontation itself. The confrontation is inevitable and definitive because the world is rapidly growing smaller as a result of the technological revolution and, most particularly, the runaway development of communications.

Because this whole world of widely and often violently disparate parts is growing smaller by the minute, the comity of nations is rushing forward headlong, willy-nilly, toward some form of more or less effective world government. It is, formally, a question of which of the two contenders, the Soviet Union or the United States, is going to be the dominant influence in forming and maintaining that government. It is also a question in the struggle itself—because the two powers involved are so different from each other—of which of them will succeed in imposing its standards, terms, and definitions on the other. As the Soviets put it, *Kto kogo* ("Who [does it to] whom")?

Lenin never wrote that the "capitalists will sell us the rope with which we will later hang them." What he did write in a memorandum of 1921 spells out the prophecy so often imputed to him:

> My own direct observation during my long years of emigration taught me that the so-called cultural strata of Western Europe and of America are incapable of coming to grips with the present situation or with the true correlation of forces. These elements must be considered deaf and dumb, and we must act toward them accordingly....
>
> In order to lull the deaf and dumb capitalists asleep we will announce (fictitiously) that our governmental organs...are separate from the party and the Politburo and especially from the Communist International. These latter organs will be presented as

merely political groupings that are tolerated on Soviet territory. The deaf and blind will believe this....

Meanwhile, we will express our desire for the immediate resumption of diplomatic intercourse with the capitalist countries on the basis of complete non-interference in their internal affairs. Once again, the deaf and dumb will believe this. They will even get ecstatic about it and open their doors so wide that envoys from the Comintern and offices connected with the party will be able to penetrate the countries in the guise of their being our diplomatic, cultural and trade representatives....

The capitalists will extend us credits that will help us support communist parties in their countries. They will supply us with the materials and technology unavailable to us to restore our defense industry, which is necessary for our future victorious attacks against our capitalist suppliers. In other words, they will work toward preparing their own suicide....

Telling the truth is a bourgeois prejudice. Lying, on the other hand, is often justified by the goal. Capitalists and their governments throughout the world, as they yearn for the Soviet market, will close their eyes to the reality of things mentioned above and, as a result, will become deaf, dumb and blind.

But in this same memorandum Lenin made an all-important point at the very beginning:

Revolution never proceeds along a straight track, with continuous expansion along the way. Instead, it is like a chain made up of outbursts and retreats, attacks and tranquility, during which time the revolutionary forces can strengthen themselves and prepare for ultimate victory....

Basing ourselves on these observations and realizing the long duration necessary for world socialist revolution to reach fruition, we must resort meanwhile to special maneuvers capable of expediting our victory over the capitalist countries.

Compare this quote with the following excerpt from a speech made in 1920 by the novelist John Galsworthy:

> It might well take five generations to remake of London a stainless city of Portland stone.... We should need a procession of civic authorities who steadily loved castles in Spain. For a civic body only lives about four years, and cannot bind its successor. I wonder if we have even begun to realize the difficulty of true progress in a democratic age? He who furnishes an antidote to the wasteful, shifting tendency of short immediate policies under a system of government by bodies elected for short terms might be the greatest benefactor of the age. For find that antidote we must, or discover democracy to be fraudulent.

These are the basic elements of the calculation made and acted upon by the Soviets: the practice of systematic deception while banking on the short memories and the greed of bankers, businessmen, and the political frivolity of nonce majorities in popularly (and frequently) elected governments. A primary point is that the notoriously short memories of the Western democracies are institutional. An equally important point is that the "wasteful, shifting tendency of short immediate policies under a system of government by bodies elected for short terms" is made to order for the media.

Until recently the Soviet Union was able to practice Lenin's formula for dealing with capitalist countries with brilliant success. Even now a good example of how this worked is provided by the American Academy of Sciences. This august body suspended its exchange program with the Soviet Academy of Sciences some four years ago when the Soviet invasion of Afghanistan more or less coincided with the exile of Andrei Sakharov (which occurred without due process even according to Soviet law) to the town of Gorky which is off limits to foreigners. In the spring of 1984 a representative of the American Academy was in Moscow negotiating the resumption of the exchange with the Soviet Academy. It is important to note that meanwhile, nothing had changed. The Soviet invasion army was still laying waste to Afghanistan and Sakharov was still in exile in Gorky. The Soviet government was about to pocket the gain of resumption of the exchange hardly four years after the indignant American rupture of the same. The American scientists simply came (after four years) to accept the new "status quo" (as the Soviets were certain they would).

But no sooner was the resumption of the exchange announced than Sakharov went on a hunger strike to be ended only when the Soviet authorities allowed his wife, Yelena Bonner, to leave the Soviet Union for badly needed medical treatment abroad (this was Sakharov's second hunger strike; his first had forced the Soviet authorities to allow his prospective daughter-in-law to emigrate to the United States some two years before). The American Academy of Sciences was acutely embarrassed by the timing of these events (as well it should have been—having been caught in the act, as it were) and announced a month or so later that the exchange just negotiated would be postponed until the Sakharov case (by this time a full-blown international scandal) had been clarified.

However, there have occurred since World War II a number of events that have disturbed, disrupted, and perhaps definitively scotched the implementation of Lenin's formula—which formula amounts to a sort of political judo trick, in which the weight and momentum of capitalism are used to overthrow capitalism by means of a feint: détente—or the repeated hoodwinking of the "deaf, dumb, and blind." The first of these is the founding of the state of Israel and its emergence more or less recently as a major regional power. The basic policy of *aliyah*, the ingathering of the exiles, in itself was bound to draw attention to the 3 million Jews in the Soviet Union, the more so since—and this is an all-important point—the *aliyah* proved to be no great attraction to American Jews. These preferred to make their contributions by donating financially to the new state and extending moral and political support. The result has been that the United States of America has acquired a highly professional, professionally vociferous, knowledgeable body of steadfast observers and trenchant critics of the Soviet Union—and this even before the arrival of the 100,000 Soviet Jews whom the Jackson-Vanik Amendment enabled to emigrate from the Soviet Union. Without them, without the "preemptive vigilance of the Jewish-American lobby," Lenin's formula might well have worked indefinitely. But the Jews have a collective memory, and for all their savoir vivre they are not given, either as a people or as a group, to losing themselves in "Utopia now!" Without them the American government and people would not pay a tithe of the attention they now pay to the Soviet Union.

The importance of the appearance on the international literary and political scene of Aleksandr Isayevich Solzhenitsyn has already been mentioned. Yet it would be impossible to exaggerate the significance of the man and his works within the context of the Soviet-American confrontation and the application of the Lenin formula. Solzhenitsyn stamped "gulag" on the forehead of the Soviet system once and for all. A corollary of this stigmatization is the knowledge that an appreciable part of the produce of the Soviet Union offered for trade is the work of political prisoners and of forced labor at large.

The appearance in Poland of the trade union Solidarity, even though suppressed by the Polish government, has resulted in a stalemate standoff between people and government in Poland, with the Catholic Church siding with the people but offering itself as intermediary between the two sides. On the international labor scene, particularly in the International Labor Organization (ILO), the development and suppression of Solidarity have had a tremendous effect, resulting in the formal investigation by the ILO of the Polish government's action vis-à-vis Solidarity, the subsequent withdrawal pro tem of the Polish government from the ILO, and the reprimand of the Soviet Union and Czechoslovakia for failure to observe the conventions their respective governments had signed. The

Soviet Union and several of its East European satellites
are on the verge of being outlawed by the International
Labor Organization.

The election to the throne of St. Peter of the Polish
cardinal Karol Wojtyla changed the landscape of superpower confrontation as perhaps no other event in
our time. Wojtyla's role in the development and guid-
ance of Solidarity can hardly be overestimated, based,
as it was, on his intimate knowledge of the Soviet system and its special application in Poland. Equally important, the stature and aura of the man have given
renewed hope to Catholics, Protestants, Moslems,
Buddhists, agnostics, and atheists alike throughout the
world. (Attendance in Italian churches since the beginning of his papacy has increased by more than one-
third.)

The most telling testimony to his importance as a
world figure and, particularly, a chief figure in the East–
West confrontation (elected as he was for the rest of his
life, not just a short term in office) was the attempt to
assassinate him made by Ali Agca, who later implicated
the Bulgarian government (universally understood to
be the proxy of the Soviet government) as ordering and
directing the assassination attempt. The arrest and
eventual binding over for trial of Sergei Antonov by
the Italian government in connection with the attempt
on John Paul's life have caused an international sensation without precedent. Antonov, a Bulgarian air-
lines official stationed in Rome, was under investigatory
arrest for more than a year. The Bulgarian government
struck back by arresting two Italian tourists, a man
and a woman, on charges of espionage in Bulgaria. (The
woman has since been released.)

Meanwhile, Italian and Interpol investigations concerning the network involved in the assassination attempts have uncovered a vast Bulgarian terrorist, drugs-
and-arms smuggler organization using the official
Bulgarian state transport system, consisting for the most
part of the huge truck-trailer fleet Bulgaria. These great
white truck-trailers range the length and breadth of
the continent, from the main ports of Western Europe

to their home base and back again, with goods under customs seals which the drivers can break and restore at will but which remain inviolate to the customs officials stationed at the various intervening borders. The "Bulgarian Connection" has become far more notorious than its French model, including as it does much of the Bulgarian state apparatus.

Fully as interesting as the exposés brought by the Italian state investigation, however, were the demurrals issued by various governments and agencies in connection with the charges brought against the Bulgarians and the supporting evidence—or purported lack of it. Prominent among the demurrers was the American State Department, the CIA, and the *New York Times.* But there were other Western countries likewise—the British, the French, and West German—in addition to the chorus from the East. It was as if, indeed very much as if, the Western powers had a vested interest in preserving the international presentability of the Soviet Union.

What would happen if the Italian government managed to establish a chain of evidence connecting Ali Agca with the Kremlin in the attempted assassination of Pope John Paul II? Why, the outcry of indignation and censure throughout the world would make it impossible to deal with the present leadership of the Soviet Union—notwithstanding the intervening demise of Yuri Andropov, the man (as the then head of the KGB) most likely to have been involved in the actual command function if such were the case. Indeed, the attitude of the American government toward Konstantin Chernenko and his colleagues in the Politburo would have to be precisely what the attitude of the Soviet Union leadership toward Ronald Reagan and his colleagues at the helm of the American government already is.

Here it is interesting to consider the double standard automatically involved in the appraisal of the Soviet and American governments. To the Soviet government, particularly for its internal consumption, Reagan and his administration represent little short of the devil and his chief hellions incarnate. (Reagan is frequently compared with Hitler in the Soviet press.) There is a good deal of sympathy with this point of view in the mainline American press. Even so, the adverse treatment of the American government in the media of both the East and the West would be as nothing compared to the storm of opprobrium that would ensue if the case against Antonov were proved.

It is bad enough as it is. It is incontrovertibly established that Agca spent several weeks in Sofia in a luxury hotel, Vitosha, notorious for its connection with the DS (Darzhavna Sigurnost), the Bulgarian equivalent of the KGB. It is also a fact that Agca's report to the Italian judges of Lech Walesa's sojourn in Rome was more accurate than the report on the same event furnished by the SISMI, the Italian military intelligence service. Claire Sterling, the reporter perhaps most knowledgeable on the attempted assassination of the pope, avows in her book *The Time of the Assassins* that Agca's involvement in a plot to kill Walesa while the latter was in Italy has already been firmly established by the Italian authorities. The attempt on Walesa was aborted because of a last-minute change in the Polish labor leader's plans. But Agca demonstrably tried to kill the pope, and the connection between the pope and Walesa is clear.

The question of *cui bono* ("who would benefit") points directly at the Soviets. But it is possible that the Italian authorities are deliberately proceeding at a snail's pace on the reckoning that by the time the trial is held and a verdict is brought in, the present top Soviet leadership will have departed the scene. Claire Sterling had the satisfaction of writing the story on the Italian state prosecutor's report which appeared on the front page of the *New York Times*, Sunday, June 10, 1984, edition under the headline BULGARIA HIRED AGCA TO KILL POPE.

The Polish standoff has been mistaken by the world public for a solution. The Polish problem has not been solved, let alone resolved. The lack of a Polish solution or resolution has baffled the Soviet leadership. It was the continuing state of flux in the Polish situation that posed the problem of massive defection at the Los Angeles Olympics. The Soviets conceivably could have coped with the ever-present risk of defection among their own athletes—even in the face of an American refusal to abridge the right of political asylum for the duration of the games. But with the Poles (whose hatred of the Soviets has its own peculiar force) they never had a chance.

Chapter XXII

Another event of decisive importance in the confrontation of the Soviet Union and the United States is really a process extending over the period since World War II. This is the unequivocal failure of the Communist work ethic. The newspaper *Soviet Russia* on May 31, 1984, published a curious discussion, including several letters from readers, centering on "points of view concerning the ruble that is not earned during regular work hours." This was an at times rather vehement presentation of the pros and cons of moonlighting, of earning money on the side in addition to one's regular salary. The language used was for the most part pejorative since the practice is officially frowned upon, although it was freely acknowledged that the practice is very widespread (as it would have to be to account for some 30 percent of the gross national product).

The fact is that everybody in the Soviet Union—except outcasts and/or dissidents who are declared parasites—has to have a regular job for which he or she receives a very small salary (the national average is about 185 rubles a month). A glaring exception, of course, is the *nomenklatura*. In order to live just a little bit better than the helots who form the basis of Soviet society, it is necessary to have a second job or do some some sort of work on the side. There are no statistics kept on moonlighting, but it seems fair to say that the percentage of workers who earn money by some means in addition to their regular salaries is somewhere between 15 and 40. It is perhaps even higher.

The point that emerges from the discussion in *Soviet Russia* is that in all too many cases regular employment is treated (and neglected) like a sinecure, while the work that brings extra money receives the lion's share of the worker's attention, energy, and initiative. Arnold Beichman, a scholar and publicist who has studied the subject for decades, avers that "20 percent of Soviet workers never show up for work on a given day—a sort of daily national strike." There is a Hungarian joke to the effect that a visiting English trade unionist took the Hungarians to task for not following the example of Solidarity in Poland. "My dear sir," said a Hungarian worker, drawing himself up, "I will have you know that the entire Hungarian *modus operandi* is tantamount to a strike!"

One of the suggestions repeatedly made (and just as often denounced) in the letters from readers of *Soviet Russia* was to set up a control system of all family budgets so that families spending more than their income from salaries for regular work hours could be brought to account.

What is striking in the debate is the semantic difficulties the Soviets encounter in trying to come to terms with the concepts and categories they themselves have created and sought to assert. This is especially true of market transactions. "Whoever considers," wrote one irate contributor, "that income from the sale on the market of his own produce does not constitute earned income (by honest labor, one might interpolate), that person has no conception of work in the sense of personal, supplementary economy."

Somewhere in Soviet mythology the whole idea of husbandry has been lost. "Some of our readers," the newspaper continues, "describes the great expenditure of labor which it is necessary to invest in a vegetable patch or a garden before there can be any produce to take to market." But then, one regular job is not necessarily very much like another. A Muscovite woman writes: "I know a technician who works in a polyclinic for a salary of 150 to 160 rubles a month, but who lives on an income of much more than 1,000 rubles a month from his private practice. But in the polyclinic his picture hangs in a place of honor as a model worker. And although all this is plain for everyone to see, people pretend to take no notice." Another disaffected writes from Vladivostok: "One acquaintance of mine has access to alcohol and other spirits. On the basis of this access he has built himself a dacha. Another has access to building materials and has built himself a house. A chauffeur uses the automobile entrusted to him to go on his own private errands. Once these people lived poorly and did without many things, and their families were large. But now? Now they have a lot more money." Balzac put it succinctly: *"L'avarice commence où la pauvreté cesse"* ["Greed begins where poverty ends"]. A great many of the letters were summed up in the question, "For whom are expensive pieces of jewelry destined? An honest worker can hardly permit himself to buy a luxury item at a price of from 10 to 15 thousand or even 25 thousand rubles." Some found that it was wayward even to produce such articles. Attention was drawn to the fact that "not infrequently the very presence in a display window of such expensive articles of luxury exerts a corrupting influence on many young people and leads to a deformation of their values." One is reminded of Simone de Beauvoir agonizing over the proposition of taking a vacation trip when millions of workers were without the means to do so.

For the Soviets the central problem remains that of

awakening the interest of each worker in applying himself, his energy, and his initiative to his "basic" work—that is, the work the Soviet government assigns him, not to his earnings from side jobs. The conclusion of the article points out that this is not merely a question of economics and jurisprudence but also one of education and ideology. "We are conducting a discussion," sums up the newspaper, "about man, about his system of values, about the formation of [his sense of] his needs—not so much about the declaration and taxation of incidental income or the form of investigation thereof."

Soviet economists may soon rediscover Adam Smith. But however soon they do so, it will be too late. It is not that the Soviets, after some sixty-seven years, are back at square one. The grand experiment has very clearly failed. They are no longer on the shore of a great discovery. The tide has turned, and they are being carried out to sea. In sixty-seven years the Soviet Union has failed to produce one single item—let alone an entire line of wares—that has achieved anything remotely resembling a breakthrough on the international market. Economically the Soviet Union is the great negative example of our time. The news of this fact—despite all the Communist good news and the capitalist bad news—has managed to get around.

So wrote Maksim Gorky, the classic proletarian author, in 1917:

Vladimir Lenin is conducting a socialist form of government in Russia according to the prescription of Nechayev: full steam ahead smack through the swamp! The people has already paid for this experiment with tens of thousands of lives and will be forced to pay with still more. This tragedy does not disquiet the slaves of dogma of Lenin and his comrades. For him life, with all its complications and entanglements, is something foreign. He does not know the masses of people, he has never lived among the people. But he knows perfectly well from books how to cause an uproar among the masses of the people, how to incite the instincts of the people. The working class for him constitutes the same element that ore does for the metallurgist. He works like a chemist in the laboratory. Only, a chemist works with dead materials and produces splendid results for living people. Lenin does just the opposite.

The working class must understand that it is being made the subject of a horrible experiment which will destroy the best that is in the working class and for long years will postpone the normal development of the Russian revolution.

Perhaps the event that has done most to discredit the Soviet Union in the eyes of the civilized world in recent years is the appearance on the international political scene (followed by his disappearance) of Andrei Dmitrievich Sakharov. In his Nobel Peace Prize address, delivered by his wife, Sakharov said that "international trust, mutual understanding, disarmament and international security are inconceivable without an open society with freedom of information, freedom of conscience, the right to publish and the right to travel and choose the country in which one wishes to live." In singling out the closed society as in itself a threat to world peace, Sakharov put his finger on the basic problem.

Nothing that has happened since Stalin's show trials in the 1930s has exposed the Soviet Union to such severe and persistent censure as the case of Andrei Sakharov and his wife. The Soviet government has revealed itself as both obtuse and malicious in its treatment of an aging and ailing married couple. It has acted as though the entire structure of the Soviet state were directly threatened by two old and infirm—and totally isolated—dissidents.

There are reasons for this. The Soviet Union, a state that by its arbitrary insolence invites calumny at every turn, erects a criminal code that includes calumniating the Soviet state. It does this in order to imprison, exile, or deport those who vociferously oppose it. It then expresses outrage when those it deports fight back from their emigration, having meanwhile managed to enlist part of the public opinion of the countries in which they reside.

In the democratic West opposition is regarded as an integral part of government, indeed as essential to viable government. And this is the point. Because it does not tolerate opposition, the Soviet form of government is not viable. It rids itself of its natural opposition via the grandiose political sewage system of the gulag plus the exile of prominent members of the opposition to the West.

In the West the opposition continues with the difference that, being abroad, it has become international. Thus an internal affair of the Soviet Union becomes an international affair because of the nature of the Soviet system and the measures that its government, in its desperation, sees itself forced to take. In effect, the Soviet Union exports its unviability to the comity of nations at large. This is a kind of internal interference in international affairs.

There is a truth about the Soviet Union which the Communist press has always carefully concealed and the Western media have never grasped in anything like its full scope and intensity. It is a truth that is well illustrated in a commentary broadcast by Radio Liberty in mid-year 1984. The occasion for the commentary was an announcement in the Soviet newspaper *Izvestia* that families with more than two children would receive a "personal telephone" with no waiting period. To this the commentator, Sergei Yushin, made the following observations:

"If we take into account that the waiting period for the installation of a personal telephone in Moscow covers several years and for people living in the provinces a full decade, then the game may be worth the candle. We must not forget that this country is at the tail end of all the developed countries of the world in the number of telephones per thousand inhabitants. The United States has from ten to twelve times as many telephones by this reckoning as the Soviet Union. But will the enticement serve to increase the birth rate among

Muscovites as well as the residents of other cities and areas of the country? Alarmed by the diminishing birth rate, Soviet leaders have already taken a series of measures to stimulate its growth. Such measures include supplemental funds for each child, differentiation of taxation in accordance with the size of the family, priority allotment of living space for large families.

"Nevertheless, the problem of the birth rate is still very much in evidence on the pages of our mass publications and specialist journals. Above all there is the intriguing question—will there be a rise in the standard of living in the Soviet Union? The standard of living of Soviet people, without any doubt, has risen in comparison with that of the year 1940, for example. However, in 1940 the number of births per thousand inhabitants was thirty-one and two-tenths, but in the year 1970, a year that can be regarded as marking the all-time high in the standard of living of the Soviet people, the number of births per thousand inhabitants was all in all seventeen and four-tenths.

"The experience of the more developed countries of the world shows that between the growth in the standard of living and the birth rate there is no direct interdependence. Rather the opposite is true. The richer the Western countries have become, the more they display a tendency to a reduction of the birth rate....At present in this country in addition to a lowering of the rate of growth of the population there is a very considerable rise in infant mortality. This rise in infant mortality, according to foreign demographers, is caused by the poor state of Soviet health services and also by increasing alcoholism....But poverty is not only the continuous lack of this or that product, not only the low quality of goods and wares, not only the rudeness of service personnel, the eternal waiting lines, the humiliating scrounging for necessities—it it also a million great and small tragedies. Relatives who have grown to hate each other because they have been forced to live for decades in one room. Lovers who have parted because they could not find a place to live. Parents who pine over the children they never had because they could not permit themselves the luxury of having children since both were forced to work. The chauffeur dead because of pot holes and the poor general condition of the roads. The oldster dead before his time for lack of medicine, the worker maimed at his place of work because of a raging fever."

The Soviet empire includes sixteen national republics and more than sixty nationalities. It is a vast, sprawling complex but with no room for any except military maneuvers. There is, so goes the insight, an essential connection between the nationalities question and the human rights question in the Soviet Union. There is also an essential connection between the Soviet economic system and Soviet censorship (just as the system of free enterprise and a free press are essentially connected). It is impossible to tinker with the one without affecting the other.

According to the United Nations Universal Declaration of Human Rights, Soviet citizens (like all other citizens) have the right to know. This right gives others the right to provide them with what they have the right to know. In theory the Soviets accept this right; in practice they deny it. The Soviet Union jams all Western broadcasts at enormous expense (it costs from three to four times as much to jam as it does to broadcast). The United States and the West in general jam nobody.

In this regard the Soviet Union is very much on the defensive. The Soviets shun (indeed, they are categorically incapable of conducting) an open exchange with the West, but they seek by means of espionage to influence public opinion in foreign countries just as they seek by the same means to acquire Western technology. Hence the large and increasing number of expulsions of Soviet diplomats from Western countries. The confrontation is the classic one between a closed society and an open society. But it is also more than that.

It is important to consider that the closed society of the Soviet Union is also (and primarily) closed to the Soviets themselves. They are perpetually hamstrung by this fact in their attempts to reform the economy without loosening the sacred strictures of their policy on information. By the same token the American open society is also open to the American government. In the Grenada intervention the American government not only dealt the Brezhnev doctrine its first reverse but also, in effect, suspended the First Amendment for three days by simply not taking the media along for the ride. And this to the demonstrated delectation of the American public (thus exploding the myth—for a while—of the identity of the media with the public).

In an open society it is just as easy to cut down as to cut up. The continuing celebration of the American "public's right to know" has provided a very stark contrast with the whole style and structure of the Soviet system, in which the public has no right to know anything.

The searchlight on Watergate threw into indelible relief the double standard applied by the world to the American and Soviet systems. The demands which were made and met in the Watergate scandal forced the American liberal left to revise—at least in good part—its attitude toward the Soviet Union. Watergate even constrained the American government to take steps to ensure the acceptance of the article on Human Rights for the Helsinki Agreements, and to deliver an ultimatum to the International Labor Organization: Either drop the double standard as applied to labor relations in East and West or forgo American membership and the Americans' 25 percent contribution to the financing of the organization. The threat helped.

It may well be that the suspension of the First Amendment for the first three days of the Grenada intervention will be used by the American governments in future as a precedent. In its May–June 1984 issue, the magazine *Freedom at Issue* in an article entitled "Press vs. Government" deals at length with the problems posed by the Grenada suspension. The article concludes that the newsmen were not invited by the government to accompany the troops employed in the intervention because the relationship between them had deteriorated since the war in Vietnam from adversarial to inimical, that the government had become convinced that the media were "not on our side."

The American press has certainly made it clear over the past forty years that it is not on the side of the government; it is not supposed to be; it has no desire to be. This being the case, a military commander cannot be impugned—morally, ethically, or anyhow—for not wishing to take a journalist into his confidence on the eve of a major military operation. The odd thing is that in a war there are only two sides. As Howard K. Smith put it in the interview quoted earlier, "The American army provided everything: They provided transportation to the battlefield; they let you put your cameras over their shoulders to take pictures of what they were doing." But no journalists were there to see what the North Vietnamese were doing. (As Solzhenitsyn asked at the beginning of his press conference in Stockholm, "Gentlemen, where were you when I needed you?")

The Americans are not at war with the Soviet Union, but they are in a sort of international, interdisciplinary obstacle race with the Soviets. It happens to be impossible to run a race objectively.

This fact places a double burden on the West. The war of words and images in the media will be fought out in the West by the West, with the Soviet Union adding a nudge here and there, leaking or withholding information as it sees fit in order to guide the controversy along lines favorable to itself. So far Soviet propaganda, with the categorically predetermined help of the Western media, has succeeded in preserving the public image of the Sandinistas as idealists.

In the media struggle between the Soviet Union and the United States for "the hearts and minds of billions of people on our planet," as that transient phantom Yuri Andropov put it, there occurred an event toward the end of June 1984 that may prove to be an ideological watershed. This was a conference on international terrorism in Washington, D.C., sponsored by a newly created private research group called the Jonathan Institute (in memory of Lieutenant Colonel Jonathan Netanyahu, who was killed while leading Israel's 1976 successful raid on the Entebbe, Uganda, airport to free passengers of a hijacked Air France jetliner). The conference brought together a number of people who have contributed much over the years to the struggle against terrorism and totalitarianism.

In fact, the signal achievement of the conference was the smithing of the formulative link between terrorism and the totalitarian state. As Senator Daniel Patrick Moynihan of New York expressed it, "The totalitarian state is terrorism come to power." Moynihan particularized to the effect that the Soviet Union not only profits strategically from terrorism but actively instigates it. As substantiation he cited the Italian investigation into the 1981 attempt on the life of Pope John Paul II which implicated the Bulgarian Secret Service and hence their Soviet colleagues in the KGB (earlier Secretary of State George Shultz had told the conference that the Soviet Union used terrorism "to weaken liberal democracy and undermine world stability").

A few days later the Senate passed a bill declaring Bulgaria to be engaged in state-sponsored terrorism. The measure puts Bulgaria in the same category as Libya, Iran, Cuba, Syria, and South Yemen and prohibits both the State and Commerce departments from promoting U.S. trade with them.

Jeane Kirkpatrick, American ambassador to the United Nations, called the Soviet Union the "world's greatest totalitarian state," adding that it was the principal supporter and sponsor of international terrorism as a form of political action. The Soviet Union, she said, discovered in the early sixties that it could gain influence in the Western Hemisphere by supporting "small bands of violent men, technicians in violence... in their effort to win power by violence." She went on to say that the Soviet Union and its allies had labeled these groups "national liberation movements." Furthermore, "their acceptance as legitimate by and inside the United Nations is as good an indicator as any of the moral confusion which has come to surround the use of violence, the choice of violence as the method of political action... the instrument of first resort.... Where traditionally states are seen as having a monopoly on the legitimate use of violence, United Nations majorities today see liberation movements as having a monopoly on the use of legitimate force." Governments seeking to repress the violence of national movements are cited for human rights violations. "In this view," said Kirkpatrick, "a society has no right to self-defense against the armed bands in its midst." Here we have a striking parallel to the tendency of Western democracy to relinquish capital punishment as a last resort of governmental control.

The same conference featured a panel of journalists and writers specializing in the study of terrorism. Of these Arnaud de Borchgrave emphasized that "the links between the Soviet KGB...and its proxy services in Eastern Europe and Cuba and its client services in Libya, South Yemen and Syria...and various international terrorist groups...has [sic] been the key story of our time. I remind you," said de Borchgrave, "that Dr. Andrei Sakharov in his political testament in the spring of 1980 warned us to take these links very seriously indeed, but the media did not heed that warning."

Shortly after World War II the surviving members of the German resistance movement responsible for the attempted putsch of July 20, 1944, formulated the theory of the illegal state, positing the right of the citizen to seek to overthrow such a state. Dr. Sakharov, in his turn, has had demonstrated by his fate at the hands of the Soviet state his contention that that state is illegitimate and illegal. In totalitarianism the public domain is the province of the state—by law. But the Soviet government made the mistake of removing first Dr. Sakharov and then his wife from the public domain not by due process of law but arbitrarily by coercion. No one—aside from a few Soviet officials—knows where the Sakharovs are. The son of Mrs. Sakharov, Alexei Semionov, has publicly offered a reward of $10,000 to anyone who can manage to contact the Sakharovs or establish their whereabouts, thus adding the last touch to a situation that was already clear. The Soviet government, in its headlessness, has blundered into the crime of abduction. Add kidnapping to government by ambush.

The challenge mounted by the Soviet Union against international bourgeois imperialism has failed. In mounting the challenge, the Soviet Union has managed to ruin its economy and to cause untold and untellable suffering to its peoples. But the paradox is that the failure of the Soviet challenge constitutes an even greater problem for the West than the original challenge itself. Not that there is a heightened danger of war: The war scare is a Soviet ploy, the residue of the peace campaign that went sour. (And in any case, the great Soviet specialty—at home and abroad—is the gasconade of fear.) But the fact is that it is more difficult to help the Soviets than to fight them. The Soviet Union is a slum empire full of intensely unhappy people caught in an exceedingly complicated crisis. In attempts to help them any slackening of the "preemptive vigilance" that is necessary in dealing with Soviets will simply reactivate the Lenin formula in which the hangman's noose is sold on credit at a low interest rate.

Does all this mean that the Soviet Union is falling apart? "It is not to be imagined," wrote Edmund Burke some 200 years ago, "because a political system is, under certain aspects, very unwise in its contrivance, and very mischievous in its affects, that it therefore can have no long duration. Its very defects may tend to its stability, because they are agreeable to its nature. The very faults in the constitution of Poland made it last; the *veto* which destroyed all its energy preserved its life. What can be conceived so monstrous as the Republic of Algiers, and that no less strange republic of the Mamelukes in Egypt! They are of the worst form imaginable, and exercised in the worst manner, yet they have existed as a nuisance on the earth for several hundred years."

The Right Honorable Member of Parliament for Bristol was seldom completely wrong.